Finding Elizabeth

Chris Campbell

Shawn Smucker

Cover design by Gentry Lusby.

Bookmark reprinted with permission of Freedom In Christ Ministries, USA.

To the Girls hoping to be found

Who I am in Christ

I am accepted.

I am a child of God. (John 1:12)
I am Jesus' chosen friend. (John 15:15)
I am holy and acceptable to God. (Rom. 5:1)
I am united to the Lord and am one spirit with Him. (1 Cor. 3:16)
I have been purchased with a price. I now belong to God. (1 Cor. 6:19, 20)
I am a part of Christ's body, part of His family. (1 Cor. 12:27)
I am a saint, a holy one. (Eph. 1:1)
I have been adopted as God's child. (Eph. 1:5)I have been bought back (redeemed) and forgiven of all my sins. (Col. 1:14)
I am complete in Christ. (Col. 2:10)

I am secure.

I am free forever from punishment. (Rom. 8:1- 2)
I am sure all things work together for good. (Rom. 8:28)
I am free from any condemning charges against me. (Rom. 8:31f)
I cannot be separated from the love of God. (Rom. 8:35)
I am hidden with Christ in God. (Col. 3:3)
I am sure that the good work that God has started in me will be finished. (Phil 1:6)
I am a citizen of heaven with the rest of God's family. (Eph. 2:19)
I can find grace and mercy in times of need. (Heb. 4:16)
I am born of God and the evil one cannot touch me. (1 John 5:18)

I am significant.
I am salt and light for everyone around me. (Matt. 5:13,14)
I am part of the true vine, joined to Christ and able to produce lots of fruit. (John 15:1, 5)
I am hand-picked by Jesus to bear fruit. (John 15:16)
I am a Spirit-empowered witness of Jesus Christ. (Acts 1:8)
I am a temple where the Holy Spirit lives. (1 Cor. 3:16; 6:19)
I am at peace with God and He has given me the work of making peace between Himself and other people. (2 Cor. 5:17f.)
I am God's co-worker. (2 Cor. 6:1)
Even though I live on earth, I am actually one with Christ in heaven. (Eph. 2:6)
I am God's special project, His handiwork, created to do His work. (Eph. 2:10)
I am able to do all things through Christ who gives me strength! (Phil. 4:13)

Letter to the Reader

The story you are about to read is real in the sense that it tells a common story of neglect, abuse, and unfairness. But beyond the pain is also the truth of redemption that comes from encountering the love of God.

At times, life can be cruel and circumstances can be devastating. Sometimes it is hard to believe that God is even real, let alone loving. There are really no words to explain how it is that children are mistreated in unspeakable ways or why you may have suffered terribly at times. The world can be a very dark place.

But in the darkness, there shines a light. His name is Jesus. The reality of Jesus is this: God became a human being (Jesus) so that he could show his love in a way that could be understood. In the midst of the darkness, Jesus offers this statement with a promise, *"I am the light of the world. If you follow me, you won't have to walk in darkness, because you will have the light that leads to life."*

As you read this book, keep an open mind to the possibility that in the midst of your greatest struggles, when you felt most alone, Jesus was preventing the darkness from consuming you. He was preserving your life so that your story would be that of an overcomer and not that of a victim. This is the story of *Finding Elizabeth*. With God's grace, this will be your story as well.

Chris Campbell

CHAPTER ONE

Lizzie closed her eyes, took a deep breath, and tried to calculate how long it would take her to get back to Detroit from the small conference room on the second floor of The Hope Center, in the-middle-of-nowhere, Pennsylvania. She figured five small steps across the small conference room would get her to the door, no more than twenty steps down the long hall, a short walk down the wide staircase, and a two-minute jog to the highway through the snow. The snow wouldn't help. But from there she could hitchhike back to Detroit, maybe even get there before the end of the week, if she was lucky.

Nae will take me back, she reasoned. *He'll understand. I'll come up with something.*

Her eyes snapped open at the sound of footsteps in the hall. She held her breath and glanced around for something to use as a weapon. She would fight her way out if she had to. They couldn't force her to stay.

There was the small, square wooden table. Three filing

cabinets lined the wall inside the entrance, carelessly covered with empty, blue file folders. To her right a small coffee table had been pushed into the corner, still holding the remains of a party: twenty or more recycled candles with blackened wicks, the colorful fragments of a few popped balloons, and one of those silver helium inflatables with the words "Happy Birthday" in bright pink script.

But the footsteps passed the conference room door, faded away, and Lizzie realized she was desperately holding onto the sides of the folding chair. She took in a deep breath, loosened her grip and sighed. She even felt a slight smile touch the corners of her mouth.

What could I possibly do, paper cut someone's throat? Beat them to death with a balloon?

She glanced at the clock: 3:10. She wondered if the counselor was ever going to show up. They had said 3:00. She was sure they had. She stood up and paced aimlessly around the room, then drifted back to the chair and sat down.

Maybe I got the time wrong?

She had only been in the home for a couple of days, but everything happened on time, every time. Everything.

At that moment, the conference room door flew open, catching a few of the file folders and spilling them on to the floor. A short woman erupted into the small space, carrying a backpack over one shoulder and a briefcase in the opposite hand.

"My, my, my," she said, throwing her things on the table, then bending over to pick up the folders. "I'm sorry I'm late! I'm so sorry. It's all this snow. Took me forever to get out of the driveway this morning, and I've been running behind ever since."

She had short black hair, just long enough to be wavy, and sharp little brown eyes. Her thin lips, when they weren't chattering like a squirrel, wrinkled up in tiny mounds. When she smiled, Lizzie felt like she was being invited into an open club of friendship.

She put the folders in a pile on the filing cabinets, but they slid to the side and one fell back to the ground. She didn't seem to notice. Lizzie took another deep breath, but couldn't bring herself to let go of the sides of her chair. She wished she would have run for it when she had the chance.

I'm not here to make friends, she told herself. *I'm not here to do anything but the minimum and then get out. Anyone who smiles as much as this lady smiles can't be trusted – no one is that kind without wanting something in return. Keep your mouth shut, Lizzie.*

The scattered woman sat down across the table from her. She leafed through a thick series of files inside her backpack and then yanked one out, catching it on the zipper and nearly tearing the tab. Under her breath she hummed the tune to what sounded like a Christmas song, one Lizzie had long forgotten. It drew strange emotions to the surface, emotions that threatened to crack Lizzie's resolve. Then the woman stopped.

"You must beeee…," she held the "e" at the end of the word as her eyes scanned the contents of the file. "Elizabeth Ann Castle? That's a beautiful name."

She looked up at Lizzie, leaving room for a response, but there was none.

The name "Elizabeth" sent Lizzie reeling. No one had called her that for, what, two solid years? Maybe three? She couldn't remember. She felt small again, tiny, like a little girl answering the door, barely able to turn the knob.

Elizabeth, is there anyone home with you?

Elizabeth, where's your mother?

"Born January 14? So that means you turn 16 next month! I guess we'll have to have a big birthday bash."

3

She smiled kindly, waiting, but Lizzie didn't say anything. She stared at the woman for a moment, then looked down. A sound rang in her memory from long ago, when she was Elizabeth, the sound of a crowd of young children singing "Happy Birthday to You," but not to her, to a friend of hers at a birthday she had attended when she was four years old. The singing grew louder and louder in her mind. Lizzie squeezed her eyes shut.

Then Lizzie heard a voice, a gentle voice saying her name. She felt herself coming back, once again aware of her surroundings. She opened her eyes. She took a breath. She unclenched her hands.

"Elizabeth?" the counselor asked again. "Are you okay?"

Lizzie allowed herself the small liberty of nodding, barely nodding. She thought about Nae. Every word she said in that room would betray him. Every word she said would be a brick in the wall keeping her from going back. She tried to stare out the window, tried to escape the room at least with her vision, but the afternoon daylight was far too bright. The sun glared off the snow and left her squinting, dazed.

"Elizabeth," the counselor began, "I'm going to need to ask you a few questions."

Lizzie stared back at the table. In her mind she ran out the door, through the hall, down the stairs and jogged to the highway. Door. Hall. Stairway. Highway. She imagined the cold, the wet snow building up on the top of her shoes, melting down around her ankles.

"Elizabeth, can you confirm for me that you are Elizabeth Ann Castle and that you are 15 years old?"

Lizzie's eyes dashed around the room again. She could feel the helium balloon hovering just over her right shoulder. She heard the tick tick tick of the clock on the wall behind her. Lizzie nodded, but it was more like a tremble.

"Thank you, Elizabeth," the counselor said. "I'm Jane Walker, the chief counselor here at the home. You can call me Miss Jane, if you'd like. It's a pleasure to meet you."

Lizzie rocked forward and back ever so slightly. She took in a deep breath and let it out fast.

"Elizabeth, I would like to find out a little bit about you, just a few things that will help us move forward."

Lizzie cleared her throat but didn't say anything. She looked up at a picture on the wall behind Jane. She had gone to Sunday school when she was Elizabeth, so she knew the long-haired man with the soft blue-gray eyes and the well-kept beard. She knew his name anyway. She knew that he was Jesus.

She recalled all the old songs, and their uninvited presence in her mind surprised her. She hadn't thought of them for years.

Jesus loves me this I know, for the Bible tells me so.

Little ones to him belong. They are weak but he is strong.

Weak. She felt so weak.

Jesus loves the little children, all the children of the world. Red and yellow, black and white, they are precious in his sight. Jesus loves the little children of the world.

In the picture, Jesus had such clear skin, smooth and very tan. He was looking off to his left at something, something up in the air. She wondered what he was looking at. Was he looking out a window, too? Did he want to escape the room he was in?

"Where are you from, Elizabeth?" Jane asked.

The images of many different houses and trailers and apartments flashed through her mind. Faces. Bedrooms. So many places. Then the last place, a small apartment in Highland Park about ten blocks from the truck stop on Route 94. She thought about the walk to and from the truck stop over uneven sidewalks, the cracks filled with tiny, glittering shards of glass. The abandoned, boarded up buildings. The hungry looks of the truckers as she walked in and sat down.

"Lots of places," Lizzie mumbled. "Too many to talk about."

Jane nodded, made a few notes in the file.

"Do you have any family we can notify? Anyone who we can tell that you're here?"

Confusing thoughts of Nae swept through her mind and she blushed, shook her head no. He had always said, maybe. Maybe someday, just the two of them. Maybe they could be a family. But not now. So no, there wasn't anybody.

"So you've been here for two days now. Have you received help regarding orientation? Have you received your bedding and toiletries?" Jane asked, tilting her head to the side.

Lizzie's right foot began to tap on the ground as she caved to the pressure to talk. The discomfort of remaining quiet - and extending the session - competed with the discomfort of speaking.

"They gave me a comb."

"They gave you a comb?"

Lizzie nodded.

"My hair," she explained, almost apologetically. "My hair gets tangled."

"You do have beautiful hair," Jane said. "I bet it felt nice to brush your hair after you arrived."

Lizzie inadvertently reached up and wrapped a small piece of her hair around her finger.

"Are there any other items you need?"

Lizzie sighed and shook her head, no. Her hand drifted from her hair back down to her lap.

"I imagine The Hope Center feels like a long way from Detroit," Jane said.

Lizzie took a deep breath. She didn't want to talk about

that. She didn't want to talk about Nae or the narrow apartment in Highland Park. She didn't want to talk about it because it felt like if she did it would vanish into her past. She wasn't ready for that.

The helium balloon dropped a few inches, touched her shoulder.

Happy Birthday to you
Happy Birthday to you
Happy Birthday dear Justine
Happy Birthday to you!

Jane shifted in her seat.

"Elizabeth...do your friends call you Elizabeth?"

Lizzie shook her head.

"What name do you prefer?"

Lizzie squeezed the side of her chair even tighter.

"Lizzie," she said, the word spilling from her mouth.

Jane nodded her encouragement.

"Okay. Lizzie. I like that name. It suits you."

Jane tilted her head to the side again. When she spoke, it was in a quiet and encouraging voice.

"Lizzie, I understand that this is a difficult conversation for you. We conduct this intake session with every new girl that comes into our home. We want to do our very best to care for you. The only way we can be considerate of your needs is if I get to know you. We'll get to know each other in the days ahead, but for now, I need to collect some basic information about you that will help us get off to a good start. Does that make sense?"

Lizzie took a deep breath. She nodded. She quickly let go of her chair with one hand and pushed the balloon away from her shoulder.

Jane stood up in a rush of activity. She couldn't move just one or two parts of her body – any action required the equal involvement of every ounce of her being.

"Let me move that for you," she said, sliding around the table and untying the balloon from the chair. Lizzie involuntarily flinched away from Jane, keeping distance between them.

Jane glanced at the coffee table.

"What a mess, what a mess," she muttered, grabbing a small trash can and throwing away the used-up candles, the pieces of balloon. "There, now we can talk."

She pushed the balloon into the corner behind her where it hovered somewhere between the ceiling and the floor. Then she sat down and leaned forward, squinting her eyes as if she was intensely interested in how Lizzie would answer the next question.

But Lizzie couldn't stop looking at the balloon. It hung in the air, drifting back and forth with an almost hypnotic affect.

Kids applauding and Justine smiling through the cloud of blown-out candles. Her dad comes over behind the birthday girl and lifts her up, spins her around.

"Did you make a wish?" he asks, a serious expression on her face.

Justine nods, her eyes shining.

"Just a minute," her dad says before running to the other room and returning with a large box wrapped tightly in "Happy Birthday" paper.

Suddenly Jane's voice drew Lizzie back to the room.

"Lizzie? Did you hear the question?"

Lizzie glanced at the door. She wondered if Jane would try to stop her. Jane was a small woman. She looked soft.

She's never seen real life, not the life I know.

Lizzie tensed her body to jump up, to fight, to run.

But Jane sighed and placed her pen down on the open file, where it rolled off to the side, then slowed, then dropped to the floor. The gesture completely disarmed Lizzie. When the pen hit the floor she suddenly wanted to cry. She wanted to lean forward and put her face in her hands and weep.

"I imagine this is all moving pretty fast," Jane said in a kind voice, looking down at the table with something like grief. Then she looked back up at Lizzie. "I wonder if anyone has taken the time to explain to you what's going on?"

Lizzie pried her eyes away from the door, but they kept looking back at the balloon balancing in midair behind Jane. It felt like she couldn't focus on anything else: the door, the balloon, the door, the balloon. The window was still too bright to look through. For a moment she heard the voices again, the children singing at the birthday party.

Happy Birthday to you!

"I am sure this can all seem pretty confusing and, well, upsetting. What we're doing here today is called an intake. You're not being arrested, Lizzie. Your presence here is not meant to be a punishment."

Lizzie nodded. Jane waited a moment and then continued.

"We want to make sure that we have enough information to treat you well and to make sure that you are cared for in a way that is helpful instead of hurtful. Maybe today, instead of me filling in the blanks on this form, you can ask me the questions. Is there anything you're wondering about?"

Lizzie looked down at her hands. The light coming through the window got even brighter as the sun came out from behind a cloud. The room was warm. But Lizzie could feel the cold penetrating in around the edges of the glass.

The helium balloon was lower now but still suspended in midair as if by magic, its small string drooping.

Happy Birthday to you
Happy Birthday to you
Happy Birthday dear Justine
Happy Birthday to you!

CHAPTER TWO

"Where's daddy?" four-year-old Elizabeth asked as her great-aunt Sylvia buckled her into the back seat of the beat-up Oldsmobile.

"Psh!" Sylvia exclaimed, as if that explained everything.

Elizabeth frowned, then stared at the small plastic watch she had found at the edge of the field beside the trailer park where she lived. A huge smiling monkey filled up the entire face of the watch, and instead of hands it had two tiny, silver balls that bounced from here to there if she shook her hand.

"Look!" Elizabeth shouted to Sylvia as she pulled the car away from the trailer. "It's five minutes!"

"You poor child," Sylvia muttered under her breath.

The day was bright and beautiful, and the blue sky shone through the car windows. Sylvia didn't have air conditioning so she rolled her window down. The glorious air felt cool and fresh and Elizabeth closed her eyes. For a moment life was beautiful.

"Where's daddy?" she asked again, opening her eyes,

pushing her long hair out of her face.

"Your daddy!" Sylvia began with gusto, but then seemed to have second thoughts. When she spoke again it was in a measured tone. "Girl, you need to stop thinking about your daddy. I know he says he's going to visit, but he never does and that's not going to change. You hear me?"

"I love my daddy," Elizabeth said.

"Well, that's got to change. There's just no sense in it. No sense in it at all."

"Where is he?" Elizabeth asked.

"I wish I knew, girl. I wish I knew. Now that's enough of that. You don't worry about him no more – he's no kind of a father you'd ever want to have around anyway."

Elizabeth looked at her watch again.

"Look!" she shouted. "Now it's ten minutes!"

Sylvia gave her a sad smile.

The silver balls bounced around inside the watch, and the car passed through neighborhoods, open fields, and more neighborhoods. Finally Sylvia stopped the car in front of a clean, well-kept lawn in a suburban neighborhood. The house rose taller than any house Elizabeth had ever been in before, and she sat in her seat without moving.

"Elizabeth! Don't you hear me, girl? Hop on out now. You go in. I'm not much for small talk and besides, I've got to go pick up your mama from work."

Elizabeth slowly shook her head from side to side. No way. She wasn't going in there.

"That's where the birthday party is, Elizabeth. I didn't drive you all the way over here to sit and stare. Now get out. Get!"

She reached into the back seat and started swatting Elizabeth with her hand. The girl struggled to pop her seatbelt free, then scurried across the back seat and out of the car. She stood outside the open car door for a moment, looking in at her great-aunt.

"I'll be back in three hours. You hear that? Three hours!"

She stopped talking and stared at Elizabeth.

"Don't your mama ever wash your clothes? Good Lord, you've got food all over yourself." She sighed. "Never mind. Now get!"

Elizabeth pushed the heavy door and it just about latched. Sylvia pulled away, the car rattling and trembling. Elizabeth turned towards the house and began the long, slow trek from the sidewalk, through the lush green grass, to the huge red front door. She had never been to a birthday party before. She didn't know what to expect.

The birthday girl's name was Justine. Elizabeth had met her in the cereal aisle of the grocery store. Justine's mother was one of Great-Aunt Sylvia's former students. "From another life time," Sylvia had said, and the two women had talked for five minutes or so while the girls stared at each other. Eventually Sylvia had arranged a few play dates. She was always trying to find ways to get Elizabeth out of her own house, out of the dirt and the cigarette smoke and the constant hum of the television that was never turned off.

The first two hours of the birthday party went well. Most of the little girls played outside on the swings or in the shade cast by a small grove of trees. Elizabeth was content to play by herself in the sandbox under the playhouse attached to the swings. Occasionally she glanced over to where Justine pushed a stroller and all the other little girls followed behind in single file. But she didn't feel left out. In fact, Elizabeth felt happy.

"Time for cake!" Justine's mother shouted from the house, and the girls squealed and raced for the back door. Elizabeth stood up, suddenly self-conscious of the gritty sand on her feet and legs and bottom. She brushed herself off and then walked quietly to the house, hoping no one would notice.

Inside, the girls crowded around a table heavy with presents and a large cake with white icing and a pink candle in the shape of the number five. A silver helium balloon floated in the midst of plain red and pink and white balloons. Elizabeth had never seen so many gifts. She wondered where they all came from, wondered where in the world there was a store with that many different kinds of wrapping paper.

"Daddy's home!" Justine shouted, pushing her chair back from the table and racing through the kitchen. The other little girls sat quietly, looking around at each other. Justine's mother bustled here and there with plates and cups and napkins.

When Justine came back into the room, she entered on the shoulders of her father, like a warrior princess returned from battle on the shoulders of the king. She grinned from ear to ear, and her father stopped to spin her around once, twice, three times before gently lowering her to her chair. The girls all cheered and Justine's cheeks flamed red, but Elizabeth wasn't even looking at Justine. She was staring at Justine's father.

He was a tall man with broad shoulders. He had just arrived home from work and his tie was loose around his neck. He carried his suit coat draped over one shoulder, and he stopped long enough to kiss Justine's mother on the cheek and whisper something into her ear, something that made her cheeks take on the same blush Justine's had so recently showed. He looked around the table, and when his gaze met Elizabeth's, he stopped, smiled and winked at her.

Embarrassed, she quickly looked elsewhere.

Then a match hissed and sparkled to life. The match kissed the wicks of five fresh candles and in an instant the cake glowed with birthday magic. Justine's mother started singing. Soon, all the children sang with her.

Happy Birthday to you!
Happy Birthday to you!
Happy Birthday dear Justine!
Happy Birthday to you!

Elizabeth watched as Justine blew out the large candle as well as the five tiny ones. A cloud of smoke hovered in the air and Justine's mother tried to wave it away with a paper plate. Justine's father came over behind her and lifted her up.

"Did you make a wish?" he asked, a serious expression on his face.

Justine nodded, her eyes shining.

"Just a minute!" he said, placing her in her seat, walking into the other room, then returning with a large box wrapped tightly in "Happy Birthday" paper.

"This is for you," he said, motioning for her to open it.

All the girls slipped out of their seats and moved around to Justine's side of the table. They wanted to be the first to identify the gift. Even Elizabeth left her seat, and she, too, walked around the table towards Justine. But she was content to stop at the back of the crowd. She didn't need to see the present. She leaned in close to Justine's father, where he stood watching his daughter open the gift he had brought for her.

For a moment, she pretended. She pretended that he was her father, that this was her party, and that soon he would pick her up and spin her around. She closed her eyes and smiled. She could picture it.

Great-aunt Sylvia pulled the car up outside the trailer and turned her head as far as she could.

"Run on in, girl," she mumbled. "I've got no time to go inside. Have to get to work. Someone around here has to work."

Elizabeth climbed out and the car was heaving over the

speed bump and turning the corner before she even got up on to the small porch. Her mother had stapled Christmas lights to the decaying hand rails (in one of her better moments), and they were never turned off. In the dim light of that summer dusk, the lights let out a hazy glow. Elizabeth propped the screen door open behind her, turned the knob on the front door, then pushed against it with all her weight. It opened on the third try.

Inside, all was dark.

"Mom?" Elizabeth called out. "Mom?"

No answer. She stretched up on her tip-toes and turned on the kitchen light. A small table was pushed against the wall beneath a window covered in cardboard. It was hot, and fans of various shapes and sizes were propped in every window. The yellow refrigerator was empty. The glass face of the stove was broken, and the jagged glass looked like sharks teeth. Elizabeth walked over to the couch and sat right in the middle, turning on the television.

Headlights pulled up outside the trailer and stopped. She heard two people shout at each other, then silence. Then the car pulled away. She sighed, relieved, hoping her mom wouldn't bring anyone home. What would her dad do if he found out? He'd never come back! Even at four years old, she felt a large measure of responsibility when it came to keeping her mom in line.

Elizabeth turned the television up real loud to scare away anyone who might think about coming inside. The sound also made her feel braver than she was, and with the loud voices of cartoon characters as her backup, she walked back the narrow hallway towards her mother's room. She never knew what she might find, but she wanted to get it over with while a little bit of light still crept in around the corners of the cardboard and the fans propped in the windows.

First, she pushed open the bathroom door and found the usual mess, but no one was in there. Then she peeked into her own room and turned on the light beside her bed, a mattress on the floor. She felt safe in there because she could lock the door, but first she knew she had to check her mom's room. She left the light on and the door open, then crept back the hall to the last door.

She pushed it open. The room had its own bath, but the light was off. A huge dresser sat in front of one of the windows, and a few unpacked cardboard boxes sat at the foot of the unmade bed. The covers and sheets were twisted up like a snake and the fitted sheet had come loose from one of the corners revealing the naked stains on the mattress.

No one was there. Her mom wasn't home. She sighed with relief before walking back out to the living room, turning up the television even louder, and then walking back to her room. She looked at her small plastic watch, the one with the monkey face.

"Bed time," she muttered to herself, closing and locking her bedroom door.

By the time she fell asleep she had forgotten that her mom wasn't home. She wasn't thinking about her great-aunt or how dark it was in her room. She wasn't even thinking about her watch.

No, she had one thing on her mind: the kindness of Justine's father. The way he had carried Justine into the room on his shoulder. The way his eyes had simply beamed at his daughter's happiness.

"I bet my dad's like that," she whispered to herself. "I bet my dad's just like that."

CHAPTER THREE

Jane climbed the stairs of The Hope Center. Her bag felt heavy that day, and there seemed to be more stairs than usual. Every so often she heard one of the women, girls really, pass through the house. A few of them were in the kitchen cleaning up after lunch, laughing. That was nice, hearing them laugh.

She walked down the hall and into the small conference room. She had cleaned away the remnants of the birthday party after her last session with Lizzie, wondering all along what deep-rooted memories that balloon had stirred to the surface. Obviously something.

Jane sat down and sighed a weary sigh, then pried through her bag for Lizzie's file. She had ten minutes to use up until her session with Lizzie began. She set the pale blue file on the table in front of her and gently opened it. The front page was mostly blank, with only Lizzie's full name and date of admission into The Hope Center. Jane turned to the second page - this was what she had written after their first session, only a few days before:

Mental Status Exam Report

Elizabeth (Lizzie) is a 5'7" adolescent, white female of average weight. At the time of the interview, she had a flushed complexion and one scar just under the ledge of her chin - only noticeable if she looked up. She presented herself in a quiet, distant manner during the interview, was perhaps dressed a bit cold for the season, and refused to answer most questions. She was not confrontational but withdrawn. She did not make eye contact. Psychomotor skills were sharp, perhaps over-alert. No other unusual physical characteristics or speech patterns were noted. No evidence of current drug or alcohol dependence was observed.

During the interview, Elizabeth alternated between alert and distracted. While not formally assessed, she appears to have average intelligence. Memory function difficult to assess based on limited response, although a birthday party balloon seemed to cause deep emotional triggers. Abstract thinking difficult to assess.

Flow of thought difficult to assess based on limited interaction. Seemed easily distracted by particular items in the room.

Thought content appeared to be overactive. Difficult to pull her outside of herself. No evidence of hallucinations, delusions, or paranoia was apparent. She remained silent and deeply distracted throughout the interview. No compulsions or obsessions were observed.

Sensory motor and perceptual processes appeared within normal limits. Elizabeth was able to adequately write her name and date of birth on a sheet of paper. There was no evidence of hand tremor, auditory, or perceptual difficulties.

During the interview, Elizabeth displayed a moderately depressed mood. She did not smile or show signs of humor. She only said two complete sentences during the interview, and her voice tone had monotone qualities. She sighed many times during the interview. No history of manic-like symptoms was reported.

Elizabeth seems to possess impulse control and judgment, however, at various points during the interview she exhibited signs of wanting to flee.

Jane gave a wry smile as she read back through the interview notes. So little information. She'd have to dig in a bit more.

The door opened and Lizzie walked in, quiet and staring at the floor.

"Good afternoon, Lizzie," Jane said, looking at the report, trying not to put too much pressure on Lizzie with her gaze or her tone.

"Hi," Lizzie said in a tiny voice.

Well, that's a start, Jane thought to herself.

"Your hair looks nice," Jane said. "Is your room and bathroom working out for you here?"

Lizzie nodded.

"How have the last few days gone for you?" Jane asked.

"Okay," Lizzie said, and by her tone Jane could tell she was at the edge of her comfort zone. She didn't want to lose her, so she stopped talking for a few moments.

Lizzie sat down and held on to the sides of her chair as she had during their first interview.

"Is there anything you need right now?"

Lizzie shook her head, no.

Jane paged through the rest of the file, then closed it and put it into her bag. She pulled her yellow, lined notepad and her blue pen from the front flap, set them on the table, and smiled at Lizzie. She hoped Lizzie noticed the blank page. She liked the idea of starting with a blank page.

"Lizzie, there are a few questions I need to ask you so that I can finalize the intake report. Some of them are easy questions. Others might require a little work on your part, but I am sure we can successfully work through them together. Are you ready to begin?"

Lizzie nodded, but her eyes started to dart around the room

again: the window, the clock, the floor, the door. Jane quickly glanced through the questions and tried to rearrange them in her mind so that she could begin with the least threatening topics.

"Let's start with something fun: what do you enjoy doing? Do you have any hobbies? Any activities you'd like to talk about?"

Lizzie took a deep breath and stared at the table. To Jane's surprise, she opened her mouth and started talking. Her voice came out slow and deliberate, a child's voice.

"Well, when I was small I liked riding bike. Pretty much my favorite thing. When I got older I got interested in doing hair, makeup, that sort of stuff. I used to do the girls' hair at the house...."

Her voice cut off, and her lips pressed together in a straight line.

"I can tell you like to do hair," Jane said quietly. "Your hair is beautiful. What got you interested in that?"

Lizzie shrugged.

"I was just always good at it."

Jane wrote a few notes on her notepad.

"That's very good, Lizzie. Thank you for sharing that with me."

Lizzie shrugged again, but the tiniest smile touched the corners of her mouth.

"How about your employment history, Lizzie? Have you ever had a job?"

Images of cash flashed through Lizzie's mind, twenties folded over and stuffed into her jeans pocket. Wads of cash in Nae's hand as he flipped through the bills. A thousand wallets in the hands of a thousand different men.

"I was too young to work when I ran...when I left. Never had a real job in my life."

Jane nodded and scribbled a few more things on the pad.

"How young were you when you first ran, Lizzie?" Jane asked.

Lizzie squeezed her eyes shut and rubbed her forehead with her hands. She leaned forward but didn't speak. It was almost as if she didn't hear the question. Jane allowed the moment to linger, and at first the silence increased the tension, but as the silence lingered the tension dissolved, like a knot loosening.

"Often young people run because 'home' is not a place of safety and peace," Jane continued. "Lizzie, does that describe your childhood home."

"You mean, 'homes,'" Lizzie murmured, but she also nodded.

"Did anyone ever hit you or abuse you?" Jane asked, hoping she hadn't crossed the line, hoping Lizzie wouldn't shut down. But to her surprise, Lizzie laughed a loud "ha!"

"Anyone? Try everyone," then suddenly she fell back inside of herself, and the voice that came out was small and lost. "I been hit a lot. But I'm not much of a fighter."

Jane put her pen down on the notepad.

"I'm so sorry," she said, and the thinly veiled anger in her voice got Lizzie's attention. "I'm so sorry you had to experience that. It's not okay that people treated you that way."

Lizzie felt tears rising and she stared hard at the ground.

"Did you hear me, Lizzie? It's not okay that people treated you that way."

Lizzie gave a hurried nod and hastily brushed the tears from her face.

"Yeah," she said. "Yeah."

The two women sat in silence for a time. They could both hear the clock ticking on the wall. The winter wind shook the storm windows, and the sun glared off the patches of remaining snow. Huge trucks rushed by on the highway a few hundred yards from the house.

"You ever been hit?" Lizzie asked, her words barely louder than the ticking of the clock.

Jane looked at her.

"Pardon me?"

"You ever been hit?"

Jane sighed, then nodded.

"Yes," she said, surprised at how difficult it was for her to voice that answer, to own that fact.

"It's no good," Lizzie whispered.

"No, it's not."

"Who hit you?" Lizzie asked, her voice still in a whisper.

"My father," Jane said quietly. "He hit me when I got too loud. And my ex-husband. He wanted everything to be perfect."

The two women sat there, their confessions swimming around them in the silence. Jane picked up her pen and started tapping it on the table.

"Do you stay in touch with any of your family, Lizzie?"

"I don't have any family. My parents are gone, who knows where. My great-aunt's got to be dead by now. She was old, old when I was a kid."

"Do you have anyone you stay in touch with? Who takes care of you?"

Immediately an image of Nae flashed into her mind. Short and stocky with black hair and a scar that ran along his right eyebrow like the outline of a mountain. She pictured him laughing when he took her shopping. She felt him embracing her, hugging her, as if she was his daughter. She missed him. She missed Nae.

But she shook her head, no. No one takes care of her.

Jane paused for a moment. She knew something was going on inside Lizzie's mind.

"Lizzie, I need for you to understand something. I want you to look at me while I say this." Jane paused as Lizzie reluctantly directed her gaze to the face of the odd little woman across the desk from her.

"Lizzie, no one here is going to try and 'fix' you. We are not in the business of 'fixing' young people. Instead, we try very hard to help young people find solutions for problems they have encountered throughout their lives. We do not want to 'fix" you Lizzie. Instead, we want to work with you to get you on the track that will lead to safety, peace and finding your rightful place in the world. Do you understand what I am saying to you, Lizzie?

Lizzie nods then looks back to the floor.

Jane continues: "Good. Now then, in order to find solutions we need to understand the problems you face and their beginnings."

Lizzie let out a long sigh and sat back in her chair. Her hands instinctively reached for the sides of the chair, for something to hold on to, but then she sighed again and folded her hands in her lap.

"Lizzie, I need to ask you to take me somewhere," Jane asked.

Lizzie looked back into Jane's eyes, not sure what she meant.

"Can you take me back to your childhood?" Jane asked. "What were things like for you when you were little?"

Lizzie's gaze pulled away from Jane's and hit the normal points around the room: the window, the clock, the door. Her leg started shaking and she held on to her chair again, something she hadn't done since she walked into that session.

"Lizzie. Lizzie, look at me. Right here. Good! Lizzie, it doesn't have to be anything major. Just small things you remember about the house you lived in or the people you know. We can start simple."

Lizzie nodded with her whole body, rocking forward and backward, forward and backward.

"Okay," she said, pushing her hair behind her ears. "Okay. Like I lived in a trailer before they took me from my mom? That sort of thing?"

"Sure, that's perfect. Anything like that."

Lizzie pushed her hair behind her ears again.

"Okay. I can do that."

CHAPTER FOUR

As much as Elizabeth tried, she could not fall asleep the night she got home from the birthday party. She lay in her bed for a long time, listening to the loud volume of the television soaking through the walls. She waited for the slam of the screen door as her mother came home alone or the sound of laughter and things crashing if she came home with someone else. But the night carried on and none of these things happened. Just the endless droning of the television, turned up as loud as it would go.

Elizabeth became more and more awake as she waited. It wasn't that she was scared – the dark didn't scare her and neither did being alone. She was often alone in the dark. But this time she began to feel anxious. It felt like something different would happen. If her mom didn't get home soon, alone or with someone else, Elizabeth felt as though something very new would take place.

By 11:45pm, this feeling kept Elizabeth so awake that she peeled back the covers and returned to the living room dragging her small, stuffed rabbit, Mr. Bunny, by one arm. Occasionally the plywood splinters reached up through the threadbare carpet and snagged him. Each time she stopped, freed him, and continued on.

In the living room she sat down in the middle of the sofa and waited for her mother. Directly above her the ceiling sagged, brown and water-stained. The television was much too loud. She had set the volume so that she could hear it in her bedroom, but now she couldn't find the remote. So she sat, first with her hands over her ears, and then with a cushion pressed up against her head. Maybe this was why she didn't hear the knock at the front door.

But she saw the knock with her eyes. Her mother had a wooden cardinal hanging from a tiny, golden hook on the inside of the door. So even though Elizabeth didn't hear the knock, she saw the cardinal bouncing front and back and side to side and realized there must be someone at the door. Her mother had told her many times not to answer the door, but Elizabeth was very bored. She even managed to convince herself that it was Justine's father coming straight over from the birthday party, that he knew she was there alone and had come to tell her she could live at their house until her mother was better.

She imagined opening the door and finding him standing there. He would pick her up and twirl her around the way he had spun Justine at her birthday. She imagined falling asleep in the back seat as he took her to that beautiful house. She imagined shouting, "Daddy's home!" every evening when he came in from work, and running through the kitchen in her slippery socks to greet him at the door. Elizabeth imagined what it would be like to be *found*; by Justine's dad or any dad, for that matter.

Elizabeth was very disappointed when she opened the door

and it was only her neighbor, Mrs. Bryant. She was a middle-aged woman with squinty eyes and a little dog she always walked around the trailer park. She never picked up the dog's poop. She was always complaining to Elizabeth's mother about all the dreadful things going on in the neighborhood.

"Elizabeth? Elizabeth, is that you?" she demanded through the darkness.

"It's me," Elizabeth said, wishing she hadn't answered the door.

"That television is keeping everyone awake! Why is the TV so loud? What's going on in there?"

"Nothing, Mrs. Bryant."

"'Nothing, Mrs. Bryant'," Mrs Bryant repeated in a mean voice. "Turn it down this instant! I will not leave this door until that racket has gone!"

"I can't find the buttons."

"The remote?"

Elizabeth nodded.

"Where's your mother? Go wake up your mother. I want to talk to her."

"I don't know," Elizabeth said quietly.

Mrs. Bryant's squinty eyes got even squintier.

"You don't know? You don't know where your mother is? How old are you?"

Elizabeth held up the five fingers of her right hand, then pulled her thumb into her palm.

"Four years old? Four years old? And your mother left you home alone? This is ridiculous. Step aside, child. I'm coming in."

It wasn't long before the police car arrived. The siren wasn't on but the lights on the police cruiser pulsated throughout the trailer park. The glow drew people from the neighboring houses like moths to a flame. Everyone wanted to know what was going on, who was in trouble and what would happen next.

Elizabeth sat on the sofa while the police officer spoke with Mrs. Bryant. The officer leaned up against the front porch railing and Mrs. Bryant sat in Elizabeth's mother's chair, as if she owned the chair and the porch and the house. Elizabeth didn't like that. It was their house, not hers. The police officer talked to Mrs. Bryant for a long time, but Elizabeth wasn't worried. She hadn't done anything wrong. Had she?

In any case, she felt certain that her mother would be home soon. She would sort everything out. Mrs. Bryant would stop squinting at her and the police officer would drive away and everyone would go back into their ramshackle trailer-homes. Elizabeth would lie down in her bed, holding on to Mr. Bunny, and she would wake up in a new, bright day and everything would be okay. Everything would be the same.

But that is not what happened.

First, the police officer asked her if she knew where her mommy was. She shook her head no. Then the police officer asked if her mommy had left a number or a way to reach her. Again, Elizabeth shook her head no. The police officer sat there for a few moments without saying a word, just staring quietly at Elizabeth. Then he told her something she'd not soon forget.

"Everything will be okay," he said. "I'll be right back."

Neither of which proved to be true.

The police officer never came back inside. Instead, about ten minutes later, a short, black-haired woman knocked gently on the door and then walked into the living room. She wore a light, tan jacket, jeans and sandals. Her face was perfectly round and she had a kind smile.

"You must be Elizabeth."

Elizabeth nodded.

"I'm Kate. Kate Newman."

She held out her hand and Elizabeth shook it carefully. She wasn't used to adults wanting to shake her hand.

"Are you scared, Elizabeth?"

Elizabeth looked down. She wasn't sure what the right answer was to that question, so she pretended not to hear it.

"How old are you, Elizabeth?"

Elizabeth held up four fingers.

"Four," she said.

"Elizabeth, you're too young to spend the night here by yourself, okay? I'm a social worker, and I know of some wonderful people who would absolutely love for you to stay with them until I have a chance to speak with your mother. Is there anything you'd like to bring with you?"

A growing sense of panic filled Elizabeth as she realized what the woman was saying. She would have to sleep somewhere else. She would have to leave her house and stay with strangers. In fact, she realized with horror that everyone here was a stranger, everyone except Mrs. Bryant.

"My mommy says I'm not supposed to talk to strangers," she said quietly.

"And your mommy is right. But you've met me now, right? So I'm not a stranger. And I'm going to take you to stay with some very good friends of mine, so they won't be strangers either."

"If mommy comes home and I'm not here, she'll worry. I don't want her to worry."

Kate Newman nodded a very sympathetic nod, and she smiled a sad kind of smile.

"We are trying very hard to contact your mommy, okay? As soon as we do we'll let you know and you can talk to her. But tonight you need a place to stay. You can't stay here by yourself."

Elizabeth nodded. She stood up and walked back to her room. She found some clothes she liked and she gave them to Kate Newman. She put on some shoes which felt very strange because it was so late at night and, besides, she still had her sleeping clothes on. Then she followed Kate Newman out to the car, dragging Mr. Bunny along by one ear.

The police lights were still flashing but no one was on the street anymore. Even Mrs. Bryant had gone back to bed once the police officer had unplugged the television. Kate Newman's car pulled away from the curb in one long, slow motion, and Elizabeth felt as though she were being swept away. She fell asleep.

They drove for about ten minutes to a neighboring small town. It was the kind of place with streetlights and stop signs on every corner. If it had been daytime, Elizabeth would have noticed how green the grass was, how some of the houses had small, white picket fences along the sidewalk, how even the mailboxes were freshly painted bright reds and greens and yellows. But she slept, and it was very, very dark.

The car stopped. Kate Newman's door slammed, and then one of the back doors opened. She reached in and pulled Elizabeth from her sleep, carried her and Mr. Bunny to the front door of a pretty, two-story brick house. She knocked lightly on the door, and the porch light came on. Elizabeth shoved her face even deeper into the crook of Kate Newman's slender, sweet-smelling neck. She felt an ache for the familiar. She wanted to go home with Kate Newman, not stay here in a house with complete strangers.

"Poor girl," she heard a voice whisper. "Is she sleeping?"

Kate Newman carried her up the stairs to a small room with a dim night light.

"Elizabeth?" Kate asked. "I'd like to introduce you to

someone, and then you can go back to sleep."

Elizabeth peered out from the safe confines of Kate Newman's neck. She was staring at the dark outline of a woman, though in the dim light she couldn't see the details very well. She was tall and thin and older than Elizabeth's mother. She had wrinkles that spread out from the corners of her eyes.

"This is Beth," Kate said. "You're going to stay here, at her house, until we have a chance to talk to your mother."

Elizabeth nodded. She was beginning to realize that quietly agreeing to things meant she didn't have to talk. Silence was an easier option than trying to think and talk like a big girl.

Kate Newman laid her down in a small bed and both women walked out into the hall. She could hear their voices talking, but she couldn't tell what they were saying. She crawled out of her bed and went over to the line of light shining through the nearly-closed door. She listened.

"...We can't find her," she heard Kate Newman say. "So it could be for a few weeks, until we establish a few things."

"That's okay with us. You know we've been waiting for a girl to foster. This is why we're here."

"Thank you, Beth. You're an angel. I'll be in touch tomorrow."

The voices said a few more things, and then the front door opened and closed quietly. But Elizabeth didn't even hear it, because she had fallen asleep, on the floor just inside the room. The thin line of light from the barely-opened door fell across her face, and she thought she had been mighty lucky to end up in the house of a real, live angel.

31

CHAPTER FIVE

Lizzie stopped talking and sat back in her chair. Her shoulders sagged and she felt for the edges of her chair again. Her eyes looked tired and sad.

"Thank you for sharing that story with me, Lizzie," Jane said. "Thank you for trusting me with that."

Lizzie nodded the way she always did, with her entire body swaying front and back. She looked through the window and wished the snow would melt. Even though it was only December, she felt an overwhelming desire for spring.

"Have you been in touch with your mother through the years?" Jane asked.

But Lizzie was back to her old silent self. Her heel went up and down, up and down, tapping a slow rhythm on the floor. Her eyes explored the room: the door, the window, the clock.

"Just a few more questions for today," Jane said. "Then you can go back downstairs."

Still nothing from Lizzie. Another sigh. Shifting eyes.

"Can you tell me about your religious background?" Jane

asked. "Do you have any religious beliefs?"

Something stirred in Lizzie. It was as if the question itself brought her back to the room, back to the surface. She clenched her jaw and held even tighter to the chair.

Jane considered her position. Lizzie had come very far during the session. She could end it now, on a good note, but Jane sensed a moment of opportunity with Lizzie. She could feel them bumping up gently against a boundary. She wasn't sure if they could get back to this exact point again. She decided to keep moving forward.

"Can you tell me how you feel about religion?" Jane asked.

Lizzie gave a short, exasperated sigh and looked like she was about to say something, but then she pulled back.

"Lizzie, do you believe in God?"

The question was like a match dropped into a puddle of gasoline. Lizzie squinted her eyes and her mouth twisted, as if she had just eaten something that tasted terrible. She licked her lips quickly, and when the words came out they were loaded down with anger and bitterness.

"God?" she asked. "God? Do I believe in God?"

She gave another short "Ha!" before continuing.

"That word means nothing to me. Nothing. Where was God when my mother never came home? Where was God when they moved me from foster home to foster home because no one wanted to keep a confused little girl? Where was God when that boy at church was abusing me, the son of the pastor? Where was God when my foster parents and the precious church turned a blind eye?"

Her voice stopped working for a moment and the look on her face turned from anger to shock. It was as if she had forgotten about that abuse, only to see it resurface in front of her. Her eyes darted back and forth. She was scared about what was coming out of her. But she couldn't stop.

"That happened in God's house. God's house!" she laughed another spiteful laugh. "If God was there, then I don't want any part of God. But I'll tell you the truth, if you want the truth. All of that happened because there's no God. There is no God. There. Is. No. God."

Her last words came out almost like a plea, a plea to Jane to believe her, believe what she was saying. She clenched her jaw and took heavy breaths. Jane let the silence rush in and fill the room. When she spoke it was with calm, evenly spaced words.

"I know that often it can be difficult to understand..."

"No!" the word burst from Lizzie on its own accord and she waved her hand at Jane as if warding off a pesky fly. "No! Stop it. I understand perfectly. Stop."

Lizzie leaned forward and hid her face in her hands, as if that would make everything right. Jane took a few quiet breaths, then came at it from a different direction.

"I'm sure you know by now that The Hope Center is a Christian organization, Lizzie. We do believe in God. We believe He loves us, all of us, very, very much. I have a few things I'd like to give you today. I hope you'll accept them as gifts from me and the Hope Center, even if you don't want to have anything to do with them after you leave the room."

Lizzie didn't remove her face from her hands. Jane couldn't tell if she was crying or simply hiding. Jane reached into her bag and pulled a few things out, then pushed them across the table towards Lizzie.

"First of all, I'd like to give you this Bible. There are some verses in there I'd like to talk to you about, but first I'd just like you to have it, to get used to having it around."

Lizzie moved her hands down so that her eyes appeared just above her fingertips. She stared at the Bible on the table, and Jane could tell there was an internal battle taking place about whether or not she would take it.

"The Bible is God's love letter to you. To you, Lizzie. In it you will see the contrast between accepting God's love and becoming his child, or fighting and striving and trying with all your might to receive the imperfect love of this world, which will only lead to disappointment."

Lizzie's hands dropped away from her face. She looked worn down.

"The second thing I want to give you is a journal to write in. I'd like you to try to write in it at least a couple times a week, but you can write in it more if you'd like, as often as you want. No one else will read it – it's your own, private journal. But if you want to read your entries to me when we meet, that might be helpful."

"Finally, I'm going to give you this bookmark to use when you're reading. Of course, it will help you keep your place. But there are also some very important messages written on the bookmark that I think would be helpful for you to examine. We can talk more about them in our future sessions."

Jane placed the bookmark on top of the journal and the Bible so that Lizzie could read it. Lizzie's eyes glanced at it, then froze as she read the topmost line. Her hands didn't move from her face, but Jane could tell she was transfixed by what she was reading.

I am God's child.

Child.

Lizzie hadn't thought of herself as a child, as anyone's child, for many, many years. Too many. From such an early age she had been expected to act grown up, to be grown up. After she ran away, she would often see children doing childish things like swinging or running or crying, and she would think to herself, *I never got to do that. I was never allowed to be a child.*

But it wasn't only that. The line said that she was God's child. In other words, she belonged to someone.

35

That was something else she had never felt. Belonging.

One of her hands slid slowly over the table, reaching for the Bible and the bookmark. She pulled them towards her and held them in her lap. She swallowed hard, looked up at Jane, and nodded a barely perceptible nod.

A few minutes later Lizzie walked the hall from the conference room to the stairs. Jane had stayed behind to tidy up the room, and The Hope Center was quiet. Lizzie's mind felt heavy, full of so many memories and thoughts. She felt stirred up, like a freshly plowed field. She needed to be alone. She needed to sit and close her eyes.

But after she went down the stairs and walked through the empty living room, past the kitchen and into the back hall, she saw Penny Worthington milling around outside her door. She sighed. She wasn't in the mood for Penny. She tried to slide by her and into her room, but Penny saw her coming.

"Hey, Lizzie, what's up?"

Lizzie gave her a flat smile.

"Not too much, Penny. What's up with you?"

"Just in between chores. You know. Same old, same old."

Lizzie nodded politely, ducked her head and tried to ease past Penny. But Penny wasn't finished talking, and Lizzie was too polite to simply walk into her room and close the door on Penny's face.

"You ever think about what you want to do when you get out of here?" she asked.

Lizzie considered Penny's question. She hadn't really. The next hour was all she could manage to think about.

"Not really," Lizzie said, waiting to see if that was the end of the conversation. Hoping.

"I been thinking about it a lot. You know, I been here the longest of anyone."

Lizzie nodded. Everyone knew that Penny had been there the longest because Penny never stopped talking about it.

"But you know," Penny continued, "at some point I'm gonna have to get on out of here, start a new life, a real life."

The thought disturbed Lizzie. Trying to start a normal life after The Hope Center? That idea totally overwhelmed her. Getting a job, a house, a car. Making friends. Having a checking account. Buying groceries. Living a normal life. With all she had been through, with everything she had done, how could she make friends? Who would want to be friends with her?

"Freedom," Penny muttered, but Lizzie could tell her mind was wandering now, perhaps thinking the same things Lizzie was thinking.

Lizzie mumbled something about needing to go into her room, and she walked past Penny and gently closed the door. The door quietly latched with a tiny click. During daytime hours, room doors were not to be closed with the exception of the brief privacy required for changing clothes.

But Lizzie desperately needed that physical sense of privacy. She needed to know no one would come into her room, at least for a few minutes.

She sat down on the floor, put her back against the door and started to cry quiet tears. Her shoulders shook but she didn't make a sound. Her small, single bed was against the wall to her right, and she had a narrow desk, straight ahead of her, over next to the window. A brown and tan carpet covered the tile floor. A single ceiling light looked down at her - she hadn't turned it on, so the bright winter light coming through the window cast dim shadows around the room.

Penny's question echoed through her mind.

You ever think about what you want to do when you get out of here?

She didn't know if a new life suited her. It all felt so

overwhelming. The more things Jane uncovered in counseling, the more aware Lizzie became of her complicated past and the shame that overwhelmed her. It was like peeling an onion, layer after layer of tears. Would it ever end?

She felt herself sliding back into familiar patterns of thought, ways she had grown accustomed to viewing the world. There was always one topic that came to mind when she wanted to give up. Where was Nae? What was Nae doing? Did he miss her? Was he looking for her? If she went back, would he finally run away with her, only her? She cried harder, knowing the answer, but not knowing what to believe.

Then she looked to her right, to the floor where she had laid down her Bible and that laminated book mark. She picked up the black, leather Bible and fanned through the pages. The names of the books were familiar, but they took her back to a painful time in her life, a time when the foster families she lived with took her along with them to church. Genesis. Psalms. Isaiah. The red letters where Jesus spoke in the New Testament. She nearly threw it into the corner, but then her eyes stumbled across one word.

Father.

She stopped. She read the words around it.

"A father to the fatherless, a defender of widows, is God in his holy dwelling" Psalm 68:5.

A father to the fatherless.

Wouldn't that be nice? She thought to herself.

She looked back at the bookmark and saw the top line again.

I am God's child, it said.

She sighed, closed her eyes and rested her head back against the door. Clearer than ever, she saw two paths before her. She could stay here and wrestle with these ideas, fight and claw her way through her sessions with Jane, find out more about what it meant to be God's child. Or she could leave. She could run again. She could find Nae and apologize and hope that he would take her back.

Then, on an impulse, she reached for the journal and opened it. She grabbed a pen and started writing. There was no heading, no date. Lizzie had never kept a journal or a diary before, so she wasn't familiar with the accepted way of doing things. She simply jumped right in and started writing.

"My First Entry" Thursday, 3:30pm

I'm not sure how writing in here is supposed to help me but Miss Jane seems nice enough and she wants me to do it so I'm going to try. Plus, talking to Miss Jane fills my head with too many thoughts and memories and maybe if I start writing about some of this stuff it will have a place to go. I don't know.

This place isn't all bad. Some of the girls seem okay. Miss Jolene is the head of the house and she's very kind. The rules are kind of annoying sometimes, like the whole thing about not closing your door, but I mostly still do what I want.

Why is it so hard for me to talk about my life? There must be something wrong with me. It feels strange when I do, and I can't decide if it's a good strange or a bad strange. There's still something in me that wants to run away, to leave this place, but *there's also a part of me that knows I need to be here. Somehow this place might be my last hope.*

She stared out the window.

It had started to snow. She stood up and walked across the room towards the light. At first the snow drifted down, taking its time, but as she watched, the storm grew heavier. Soon she could barely see to the end of the yard. Her breath steamed up the window.

That's when she saw it: her own reflection in the glass.

CHAPTER SIX

Elizabeth looked at herself in the mirror. Her light brown hair, parted in the middle, hung down in two braids. Her green eyes stared back at her, curious and thoughtful. Her soft, pale skin had an innocent quality to it.

But beneath this beautiful, child-like exterior, Elizabeth was a raw bundle of nerves and worry. This was the third foster home she had lived in since she was four, when Kate Newman had whisked her away from her old house and her old life. They had never found her mother, or at least that's what everyone said.

She didn't believe them.

And because she didn't believe them, she had run away twice. Because she didn't believe adults told her the truth, she acted out in school. And because of all of these things, foster parents were kind to her but, quite frankly, more than a little relieved to pass her on.

"She's a sweet girl at heart," they'd say to one another or to the social workers that came in and out of Elizabeth's life. "But she's a hard case. She's not well-adapted."

"She has issues," they would whisper.

So there she was, another home, another new room, another new school. Another new mom and dad, this time with two new brothers and a tiny dog named Sparky. Another new mirror.

But the same old reflection.

It was Sunday morning and her new parents had told her the night before that they would all be going to church in the morning. This was nothing new for Elizabeth. Most of the people she had lived with went to church. She was used to it. So at 9:00 sharp she walked downstairs and caught the surprised glances the adults exchanged.

This is not what they expected, she thought. *They did not expect me to listen.*

Their names were Roger and Beverly, but they insisted that she call them Dad and Mom. It was difficult for her to do that. She wished they would have given her more time. It felt like just another lie inflicted on her by adults.

We can't find your mother.

Everything will be okay.

I'm your Mom and this is your Dad.

Lies. But she went along with it. She had learned at an early age that quiet obedience was best, at least for as long as she could stand it. Then, after she reached the tipping point, after she couldn't go along with the lies anymore, after she lost her temper or broke something or shouted words she wasn't supposed to shout, things went bad. Sometimes very bad.

She sat quietly and ate a bowl of cereal. Then they went out to the car where the boys, both older than she was, made her sit in the tiny middle seat. Being so close to those strange boys made her feel panicked. She didn't like feeling their legs up against hers. She didn't like catching her "Dad"s glances in the rearview mirror. She didn't like the way her "Mom" kept turning around and giving her the same sympathetic smile.

She just wanted to be alone.

Soon they walked into a bustling little church, full of more strangers with kind, fake smiles. She stayed close to her Mom, who, without a word, walked her down a dark flight of stairs to a large basement area. The basement had high ceilings, red carpet, and three doors along the left side that led into small rooms. Elizabeth's Mom walked her to the middle room.

"Here you go, Elizabeth. This is your Sunday School class." Then she turned and walked away.

Elizabeth stood in the doorway, staring into the room. Eight other children were already in there, shouting and running in circles around the small table. Elizabeth looked over her shoulder, wondering if she still had time to escape, but Beverly was not far away. She stood there, talking to a man who looked to be in his late fifties. He was short and balding and wore his pants up high around his belly button, with a brown belt pulled one notch too tight. He nodded his head in a grim manner as Beverly spoke. Somehow, Elizabeth knew that Beverly was talking about her.

She slid quietly into the classroom and moved through the chaos to the far corner of the room, then stood there, not saying anything. One of the boys came over to her. He had brown hair bordering on red and his eyes were probing. He looked her up and down without saying a word. Then he crossed his arms on his chest and asked her a question in a withering voice.

"Who are you?"

Everyone in the class turned to stare at her. She felt her face getting flushed.

"Don't your ears work?" he demanded. "Who are you?"

Her heart raced. She couldn't control her breathing. Then

another voice entered the equation.

"Please be seated."

The children scrambled to their seats as if their life depended on it. Elizabeth remained standing in the corner.

"Good morning, children," the man said. It was the same man Elizabeth's mom had been speaking with outside the room.

"Good morning, Mr. Sanders," all the children replied. All the children except Elizabeth. He glanced up at her, then back down at a sheet of paper on the table in front of him.

"Billy Goodwin?"

"Here."

"James Severson?"

"Here."

"Jennifer Howell?"

"Here."

"Katie Rue?"

"Here."

"Laura Brown?"

"Here."

"Matthew Blair?"

"Here." That was the boy who had come up to her before class started. He turned and smirked in her direction.

"Patricia Howell?"

"Here."

"Stephen Valerie?"

"Here."

The man made some marks on the sheet.

"You must be Elizabeth Castle," he said without looking up. She nodded.

He looked up at her.

"I'm talking to you, girl. Are you Elizabeth Castle?"

"Yes," she said.

"Yes, sir," he said.

"Yes, sir," she repeated, blushing.

He looked back down at his paper.

"We do not tolerate troublemakers in this classroom. Is that understood Elizabeth?"

"Yes," she said.

"Yes, sir," he said.

"Yes, sir."

"There are three other things we do not tolerate in this classroom. Can anyone tell me what they are?"

All the children raised their hands. All except Matthew Blair.

"Laura?" Mr. Sanders said.

"Disobedience, sir."

"Good. What's number two? Charles?"

"Disrespect, sir."

"Good again. Number three?"

This time Matthew raised his hand.

"Yes, Matthew?"

"Snitches, sir."

"We do not tolerate tattle-tales in this classroom," Mr. Sanders said, nodding his head. "Why are you still standing, Elizabeth? Please have a seat."

A few of the children giggled. Matthew turned and smirked again. There were no seats.

"Sir, there are no seats," Elizabeth said.

Mr. Sanders glared up at her, as if the sound of a child speaking without permission revolted him.

"What?"

Elizabeth looked down at the floor.

"Oh, of course. Matthew, go find Elizabeth a chair."

"But..."

"No 'buts' Matthew. Just because your father is the pastor

doesn't mean you can talk back to me. Go."

Matthew groaned and left the room, returning a minute later with a folding chair that he propped against the wall. Elizabeth carried it over to a corner of the table, unfolded it, and tried to squeeze her way in between two girls.

Mr. Sanders began giving the lesson for the morning, something about how, in the Old Testament, God told the Israelites to kill not only the soldiers but also the women and children. He droned on and on about the holiness of God and how humans always fell short of God's standard.

Elizabeth tried to listen. The more he spoke, the more she imagined God up in the clouds, looking down, angry and ready to punish whoever wasn't perfect. He'd curse them with disease or hardship. Then she realized: that was her. God was punishing her for the bad things she had done in her life. She wasn't sure what she had done, but it must have been terrible because he took her father and then he took her mother and then he swiped her from her own home and kicked her out into the world. She felt heartbroken and scared and wondered what God would do to her next.

Then she felt someone kick her foot.

"Ow," she said.

Mr. Sanders looked up at her, then continued with the lesson.

Elizabeth looked across the table. It was Matthew, she was sure of it. He kicked her again.

"Stop it," she hissed.

Mr. Sanders looked up again.

"Elizabeth, speaking out of turn is disrespectful and not tolerated in this classroom."

"Yes, sir."

His voice began droning again. Elizabeth thought back through her life, trying to figure out where she had gone wrong. She had only been four when her mom vanished – what could she possibly have done to offend God at that age? Of course she had disobeyed her mom at times. And she had answered the door that night, when her mother had always told her not to answer. Maybe that was it. Maybe it was her disobedience.

Another kick under the table.

"Ouch!" Elizabeth shouted.

"Young lady, you may go stand in the corner for the rest of the class," Mr. Sanders said.

Matthew smirked at her again. She stuck her tongue out in response. Mr. Sanders leaped up from his chair, raced around the table, and, with the ruler he had in his hand, swatted her bottom three quick times. All the children sat in stunned silence. It hadn't hurt, at least not much, but the humiliation was painful. Elizabeth ran from the room.

"Elizabeth! Elizabeth! You come back here right now!"

She ran through the basement towards the steps. As she turned the corner to go upstairs, she saw a janitors closet in the dark shadows of the stairwell. She dashed over to it, opened the door, went inside and pulled the door closed behind her.

"Elizabeth! Elizabeth!" Mr. Sanders voice passed by the door, and she breathed a sigh of relief. She felt around in the dark and found a bucket, flipped it upside down and sat on it. Then, finally, she cried. She cried because Mr. Sanders had spanked her and she cried because she didn't have any friends. She cried because, even after all those years, she still missed her mom. She cried because she felt so alone. But most of all she cried because she realized she did bad things and that meant God was out to get her, and that was a very overwhelming thought for a seven-year-old girl.

Time passed. Eventually she heard the sound of footsteps on the stairway as people went from their Sunday School class up to the main auditorium. She took a few deep breaths then opened the door and tried to blend in with everyone else who was walking from here to there. In the lobby she saw Beverly waiting for her.

"How was class?" Beverly asked.

Elizabeth nodded but didn't say anything. Then the two of them went into the sanctuary and saved three seats for Roger and the two boys. Peering back at her from the front row of the church was Matthew Blair. When they made eye contact, he gave her that same little smirk, then laughed and laughed.

She wanted to run out of the church but instead, instinctively, she moved closer to Beverly. But her "Mom" wasn't the cuddling type.

"Give me a little space, dear," she said, nudging Elizabeth away from her. "There, that's better."

CHAPTER SEVEN

Lizzie pulled on her clothes and stopped in front of the small mirror in her room. She had to admit – she looked better than she had in…well, as long as she could remember. Her cheeks held color, her hair was clean and brushed, and her eyes looked clear. She had emerged from the haze of drugs and regret that had hovered over her in that apartment in Detroit. That much she couldn't deny.

But there was still something she missed. There was an empty spot inside her, an ache that wouldn't go away. She figured she just missed Nae. He had been so kind to her, most of the time. Well, some of the time. She remembered the previous Christmas, nearly a year ago, when he had taken her and all the girls shopping. Everyone had $100 to spend on whatever they wanted. Her memories of that night were hazy, but she remembered feeling happy. She remembered him putting his arm around her as she bought whatever it was that she bought with the money, a ring or a bracelet or something. Something nice.

He had been there. That's what she remembered. She grabbed her journal from where she had hidden it between the mattress and the boxspring.

What's the point in staying here if I am a terrible person?

She stared at those words, then closed the journal and slid it back into its hiding place.

She walked over to the window. The snow had fallen for the last three or four days, and it clung to the trees and covered the grass. She looked down the gently sloping hill to where the highway cut through the countryside. The Sunday-morning traffic was light, but cars still rushed by on their way to somewhere. She wasn't close enough to see their windshield wipers, but she knew they'd be squeaking back and forth as all the cars kicked up the mist from the melting snow.

Huge trucks barreled past and she wondered where they were going. Los Angeles? Seattle? Dallas?

Detroit?

She remembered her small cot in that Detroit apartment, the three or four pictures she had been allowed to tape to the wall behind her pillow. She had always hidden her pill bottle in a hole in the mattress. No one but Nae knew it was there. Sometimes, when she got back during the early morning hours, she'd check for the bottle and it would be full and she'd smile, knowing it was a gift from Nae.

She sighed, standing there at the window, watching the snow continue to fall. How she wished she could get into one of those vehicles and drive, drive, drive away from there.

Why? Why did she want to leave?

But there was a knock at her partially opened door, and she wasn't able to follow that line of thinking very far.

"Lizzie?"

It was their house mom, Jolene. She peeked her head in and smiled when she saw Lizzie standing by the window.

"Can you believe that snow? Lord Almighty! What a sight."

Lizzie couldn't help but give a smile in return. Jolene was jolly, simple and round in every way. She was an enormous lady, although she was very short, and she tilted back and forth as she walked. Her nose was rounded off and her eyes were large circles. Her hair was always tied back in a tight bun.

But her personality was soft and round as well. There were no hard edges sticking out, nothing to get snagged on. Sharp words spoken by the girls who lived in the house deflected off her, usually sent flying with a smile or a small wave of her round hands. The girls who had been there for some time eventually gave up trying to insult her or upset her. It was simply impossible. Eventually they became her greatest supporters, defending her from the meanness of the next batch of girls.

"Looks nice," Lizzie said.

"Looks nice? Looks nice?" Jolene sputtered, laughing again. "More like, looks beautiful!"

"Is it time to go?" Lizzie asked.

"That's what time it is," Jolene said, shifting in a circle, pushing Lizzie's door open behind her and shuffling down the hall, peeking into other girls' rooms, pointing out the snow to anyone who would pay attention.

Lizzie took slow steps towards her opened door, then stopped, bent over, and picked up the Bible Jane had given her, tucking the bookmark inside. She could still see the words on it, the ones that tugged at her on the inside.

I am God's child.

"Let's go, girls!" Jolene shouted back the hallway. "We don't want to be late for church!"

All eight young women fit into the back of the cold van, and Jolene wedged herself into the space between the driver's seat and the steering wheel.

"What a morning," she kept saying to herself, quietly but with great enthusiasm. "What a morning."

The young women didn't say much. A few, like Penny, had been there for months and months. But most had arrived in the last three or four weeks and were still getting used to the idea of starting over, breaking free from their old ways of living. Lizzie was still the new girl, so she sat in the front row, just behind Jolene.

"Would you believe this cold?" Jolene asked no one in particular. Then she turned the ignition and the van roared to life, cold air blowing from the vents. She pulled out of the driveway and onto the small, side road that led to The Hope Center.

As they drove, the air coming from the vents turned lukewarm, then hot. Lizzie leaned her head against the van window, then used her fingers to clear the fog from the glass. Fields and trees and the occasional house rushed by, all of it covered in a layer of white.

Once the van warmed up, Penny started talking. She always talked. She always asked questions.

"Where'd you grow up, Lori?" she asked one of the other girls. Lizzie didn't know which one was Lori, but she knew that Lori had arrived just before her. Lizzie had decided early on that, since she would run as soon as she had the chance, there was no point in getting to know the other girls. Her conviction to run away had faded a little with time, but she still had very little desire to talk to her housemates, so she spent any spare time she had in her room. But that would be ending soon: her first two weeks were up, and Jane said she'd be given chores this coming week, chores she'd have to do with one of the other girls. She'd also be expected to start attending the Hope Center's group therapy sessions.

"Jacksonville," the girl said quietly. "Jacksonville, Florida." Lizzie could tell by her short, efficient answers that she didn't want to be the center of attention.

"And where were you when they found you?" Penny pried.

"When who found me?"

"You know, these folks. The Hope Center."

"Well, I guess I was in jail in Atlanta."

Penny looked up triumphantly.

"I'm from Atlanta. Told you Atlanta was a good place."

Some of the girls laughed.

"Just 'cause that's where you come from?" one of the girls said, teasing Penny.

"I was the queen of Atlanta," Penny said dramatically.

The girls laughed again.

"Where'd they find you?" Lori asked, gaining some confidence.

"Who, me?" Penny said. "They found me in Charleston."

"Well, what was the queen of Atlanta doing in Charleston?"

The van grew quiet. No one was upset, but there was a big difference between telling someone where you were when they found you, and what you were doing when they found you.

"You know," Penny said in a strong, sad voice. "Everything."

Some of the girls nodded long and slow. A few of them even gave a deep mmm-hmmm, as if encouraging a preacher. Penny sighed and looked to the front seat.

"What about you, new girl?"

At first Lizzie didn't realize Penny was talking to her. She was too busy watching the snowy landscape race past.

"Lizzie, I'm talking to you. Where did they find you?"

"Detroit," she whispered.

"Whoa, you hard core, girl," Penny said.

"Detroit's rough, no joke," another girl said.

"Places like 8 Mile? Like from the movies?" Penny asked.

"I been to 8 Mile," Lizzie said. "But it wasn't no movie."

That quieted the girls. The van slowed and the sound of the turn signal clicked through the blast of the heater.

"Lord Almighty, it's hot in here," Jolene said. "You can't ever get it just right. First it's freezing, then it's boiling. Lord Almighty."

Jolene turned off the heater and then drove the van into the church parking lot. It was very quiet with the heater off. She drove smoothly around the lot until she found an open space. Lizzie felt sick to her stomach. She hated going into church, but not just because it was church (although that was one reason). She also disliked all the smiling strangers, all the hellos and the hand-shaking. She just wanted to be left alone. She just wanted to be by herself.

Jolene worked hard to turn her body so that her round face pointed back towards the eight girls in the van.

"We're here, thank the Lord. Through ice and snow. We're here."

Lizzie and the rest of the group followed Jolene in through the glass doors. They each received a handshake, a smile and a bulletin to read. They walked down a long hallway to the gymnasium where church was held. On Sundays the basketball courts were transformed into the church sanctuary, with black chairs in lines from the front to the back.

Jolene led the girls down one of the rows towards the back, and Lizzie came last, sitting in the seat right beside the aisle. She tapped her right foot nervously and looked around, avoiding the glance of anyone who looked like they might come say hello should she encourage them with eye contact. For a moment, she thought back to her Sunday School days in class with Mr. Sanders.

Elizabeth, speaking out of turn is disrespectful and not tolerated in this classroom.

It had been seven or eight years since she had seen him last, though it felt like yesterday. Her days living with Roger and Beverly seemed like they had happened in a dream, a dream she would prefer to forget.

Young lady, you may go stand in the corner for the rest of the class.

But she had escaped them. She had run far, and she would never have to see them again. None of them. Not Mr. Sanders. Not Roger and Beverly and their two boys. Not Matthew Blair.

Not Mark Blair.

Mark Blair.

She shuddered, felt her cheeks turn red and anger simmered deep inside. Mark Blair had started out as a weird, creepy teenager that went to her church and turned into her greatest nightmare. She wondered where he was. She clenched her jaw. She wondered if Nae would help her get revenge. She could go back to Detroit, make amends with Nae, and then the two of them could find Mark Blair and cause him a kind of pain he couldn't even imagine.

"Excuse me, Miss?"

The old lady startled Lizzie, and she looked up, but the woman only wanted to get past her to a seat in the middle of the section. Lizzie stood quietly and let her pass.

Church started and the band sang a few songs. Lizzie enjoyed the music. She loved music of every kind. She reminded herself that that was something she could talk to Jane about. That was something else she enjoyed.

When the song ended the pastor walked up to the front. Lizzie didn't care for pastors. To her they were simply men who liked to show off, men who wanted to get up in front of a crowd and sound important. But she knew the truth: they didn't know what was going on in their congregations. Of course, there were the really evil ones, the ones that did know about all the wrong their people were doing, but didn't do anything about it. Didn't do anything to protect innocent people. Innocent children.

She tried to listen, though, because Jolene had a habit of asking them about the sermon on the way home. If you could answer the question correctly, sometimes she gave you an extra brownie or a piece of cake after lunch. And that woman knew how to make a tasty desert. So Lizzie listened, in an absentminded way, hoping something important would stick without her listening too hard.

"This morning's reading," the pastor said. "Comes from Isaiah, chapter one, verse eighteen."

He does have a kind voice, Lizzie admitted. *He seems like a nice person.*

"The verse reads, 'Come now, let us reason together,' says the Lord. 'Though your sins are like scarlet, they shall be as white as snow; though they are red as crimson, they shall be like wool.'"

He stopped for a moment, and the entire church was silent. A few hundred people sat quietly, waiting.

"I thought about this verse as I drove here this morning. I thought about all the mud, all the trash along the street. I thought about the puddles and the oil stains on the road. And you know what? The snow covered all of it. 'Though your sins are like scarlet, they shall be as white as snow.' No matter what you've done, no matter where you've been, no matter who you've hurt...the blood of Jesus can cover it. He can make your sins as white as this beautiful snow."

And as the pastor led the congregation in prayer, Lizzie

bowed her head and fought back tears.

Not if you knew the things I've done, she thought. *You wouldn't ever say that if you knew where I've been.*

CHAPTER EIGHT

"Honey, stop chewing on your lip," Beverly said from the front passenger seat.

Elizabeth reached up self-consciously and touched her mouth, where her teeth had been tugging at her lower lip. Then she looked at her finger. A small spot of pink. Her lip was bleeding again.

She didn't even think about it when she was doing it, but she did find herself biting her lip more and more often. Not all week. Mostly just Saturday nights and Sunday mornings.

"Gross!" one of the boys said, the one sitting to her right. "Her lip is all bloody!"

"Here, honey, have a tissue," Beverly said. Elizabeth saw Roger glance at her in the rearview mirror, then back at the road. He was a quiet man. He worked long hours and, besides the occasional dinner that he managed to make it home for, Elizabeth rarely saw him. Except on Sundays, when he backed the car out of the garage and then sat in the driveway until everyone was ready and came running out to the car, ten minutes behind schedule.

Elizabeth wiped her lip and started thinking about where they were headed. Church. Every Sunday for the last year they had been going to that same church. Every Sunday Beverly walked her to class. Every Sunday Mr. Sanders was mean and gruff and Matthew Blair gave her a hard time. She managed to slip out every once in a while to hide in the janitor's closet. Most Sunday mornings she sat in class, wedged between two of the other girls, learning about the wrath of God and the justice of God and the righteousness of God.

Matthew Blair was harmless enough. He was mostly filled with bluster and childish behavior. She learned to ignore him, and in the back of her mind she knew that one good punch to the nose would put an end to it. But he was the pastor's son, so she didn't want to risk the consequences of a direct conflict.

Matthew Blair's brother, on the other hand, gave her a sick feeling in the pit of her stomach. His name was Mark and he was seventeen years old. He was quiet, but in a forceful kind of way. He was broad-shouldered for his age, and tall. He even had a small tuft of peach fuzz on his upper lip, something she often saw him touching with his index finger.

He gave her the creeps.

One day, when she had slipped out of the janitor's closet at the end of Sunday School, he had been standing there, staring at the door.

"What are you doing in there?" he asked in his monotone voice.

"Nothing," she said, embarrassed.

He stared at her for at least five seconds without saying anything.

"Nice dress," he said, reaching out and touching one of the straps on her shoulder.

She froze. She knew she should run or shout or maybe even

fight him but she froze, like an animal about to be devoured. Her heart started racing and she couldn't breathe. Her mouth dried up and her tongue felt swollen, like it wouldn't work even if she tried to use it.

But then he walked past her, down the stairs and into the basement, through the approaching crowd of Sunday Schoolers whose classes had all just let out for the morning. She had stumbled up the steps to the lobby to find Beverly, then walked with her into the sanctuary where they found their usual seats.

"Honey, are you cold?" Beverly had asked her. "You're trembling all over."

She dabbed her lip again and dropped the tissue on to the floor of the car as they all got out and walked into church. The same hellos, the same waiting, as Roger and Beverly got their cups of coffee, the same questions about the week. The same walk down the stairs and into her Sunday School class.

Mr. Sanders came in and the chaos died down, as it always did. Matthew seemed less hyperactive that morning. He wasn't causing any trouble, which meant Elizabeth could actually listen to what Mr. Sanders was talking about. She grew more and more curious as he spoke. She had questions that needed answering.

She raised her hand. Mr. Sanders almost looked confused when he noticed her thin little hand in the air. No one asked questions, because that was the same thing as questioning him. No one questioned him.

"Yes?" he asked reluctantly.

"Mr. Sanders, does God love everyone the same?"

"Of course," he snipped. "Of course he does."

She thought for a moment. Mr. Sanders began speaking again. She raised her hand. When he saw her he sighed an exasperated sigh.

"Yes, Elizabeth?"

"If God loves everyone the same, then why do some people have nice things and other people don't?"

All the other children leaned forward. That was a good question.

Mr. Sanders didn't look amused. He was an on-topic kind of teacher. He came prepared with a lesson plan and he did not like to be interrupted.

"Life is not about having nice things, young lady. Life is about having good things. There's a big difference."

He savored the silence that followed his answer. He thought it a rather good one.

"Is it good to have a father?" Elizabeth asked quietly.

"Of course it's good to have a father," Mr. Sanders snapped. Their back-and-forth came quicker, questions followed by sharp answers.

"Then why do all of these kids have a father and I don't?"

Silence. The children stared at Elizabeth as if seeing her for the first time. The thought that someone could live without a father didn't sit well in those six- and seven-year-old minds.

"Because...because...because   you   ask.   Too.   Many. Questions." Mr. Sanders practically shouted the last three words.

Silence.

"Besides," Mr. Sanders said. "You do have a father. His name is Roger. And you have a mother. Her name is Beverly."

"He's not my father."

"He is your father."

"He's not my father!" Elizabeth shouted.

"Yes...he...is," Mr. Sanders insisted, squinting his eyes and leaning forward.

"Then he's a lousy father!" Elizabeth shouted again.

Mr. Sanders grabbed his ruler, stood up so that his chair fell over backwards and leaned against the wall, then stormed around the table to where Elizabeth sat.

"Stand," he said.

She didn't move.

"Stand!" he barked.

She still didn't move.

He grabbed her by the shoulders and lifted her to a standing position.

"You will not talk about your family with disrespect. Disrespect is not permitted in this classroom."

Mr. Sanders' face was so red that Elizabeth thought it might pop. Or perhaps he would have a heart attack. She had heard of that before and for a moment she felt a surge of guilt. What if Mr. Sanders was about to have a heart attack and die because of her?

But he didn't have a heart attack. He smacked her with the ruler three times on her upper leg. Everyone else in the class looked even more shocked than she felt. No one said a word for the rest of the class, even when he asked them questions, even when he called on them directly by name. They simply stared down at the table, hoping to escape his wrath.

"Class dismissed," he said, gathering his things and leaving before any of the other children even stood up. Then they followed him out of the room, one by one. But one girl stayed behind: Jennifer Howell.

For the longest time the two girls sat there in the otherwise empty room. Elizabeth stared at the table, waiting for Jennifer to leave. Jennifer stared at Elizabeth, wanting to say something. Finally, she spoke.

"I like your hair," she said.

"Thanks," Elizabeth said quietly, staring at different places around the room. The door. The table. The clock on the wall.

"How do you get it to curl like that?"

"I put it in braids at night."

Jennifer looked out the door, and for a moment Elizabeth thought she was finally going to leave.

"Do you do that yourself?" she asked.

Elizabeth nodded.

"I can't braid my own hair," Jennifer said, sounding as if she wished she could.

"I could teach you," Elizabeth said quietly.

The basement grew louder as the rest of the classes were released in time for church.

"Don't worry about Mr. Sanders," Jennifer said. "He's mean. But he won't hurt you."

"But it's just so embarrassing," Elizabeth mumbled. "I hate when..."

Jennifer interrupted her.

"The other kids won't say anything to anyone about it, because they won't want the same treatment. Don't worry. No one else will find out."

The basement grew quiet as everyone made their way upstairs. Elizabeth could hear the ticking of the clock as the thin second-hand made its way around the white face.

"Wanna go upstairs?" Jennifer said, standing.

"Sometimes I hide in the janitor's closet," Elizabeth said, looking at Jennifer, not sure why she had said that.

Jennifer shrugged and was about to say something, but then they both noticed someone standing in the doorway. It was Mark Blair.

"Hi," he said, leaning against the door frame. Elizabeth stood up and the two girls took a few steps towards the door.

"Hello," Jennifer said in a cold voice.

"Maybe I wasn't talking to you?" Mark said.

Jennifer turned up her nose at him, grabbed Elizabeth's hand, and dragged the girl past Mark and into the basement.

The two girls didn't say a word about it. They walked up the steps, then parted ways and sat with their parents for the church service.

Mark waited until they were gone, then walked over to the stairs. He stopped by the janitor's closet and opened the door. He took a small foot stool and moved it to the middle of the small space, then climbed on top of it, reached up towards the ceiling and unscrewed the bare light bulb. He threw it in the trash. Then he turned, walked up the steps and entered the sanctuary.

"So what did you guys learn today in Sunday School?" Roger asked as the car pulled out of the church parking lot and ran along the tree-lined streets.

The two brothers on either side of Elizabeth ignored their dad, chattering on about the upcoming school year and the beginning of football. One of them even rolled his window down a few inches, letting a beautiful blast of fresh, summer air invade the car. Introducing the noise was also an attempt to evade his father's question.

"Put that window up, young man," Roger said. "Now, who wants to go first?"

The boys both groaned, but eventually the older one mumbled something about David and Goliath. The younger one was a talker, and he rambled on and on about Gideon for so long that Elizabeth began to hope she wouldn't even get a turn before they got home. But eventually Roger cut him off and looked at Elizabeth in the rearview mirror.

"What about you, Elizabeth? What did Mr. Sanders have to say this morning?"

She wondered what Roger and Beverly would say if she told them that Mr. Sanders had screamed until his face turned red. But she didn't have the courage. She thought she would just get in trouble all over again with them, and she didn't have the energy for it.

"We learned that God doesn't care about everyone the same. Some people, they get better things."

Roger's eyes jumped to the rearview mirror, but Elizabeth was looking out the side window. Beverly looked over at Roger. No one said anything.

"We also learned that we can't be good enough for God, not ever. No matter how hard we try."

Roger started to speak, but Elizabeth cut him off.

"Oh, yeah, and we learned that if you don't do what God tells you to do, he'll strike you dead."

The younger boy giggled at that one. The older boy looked at his father, waiting for an answer.

But Roger didn't say anything. He pulled the car into the garage and the door closed mechanically behind them. The boys jumped out and ran shouting into the house. Elizabeth sat still for a moment, then slid over from her middle seat and walked into the house, her eyes sad. She had hoped she was wrong, but Roger's silence confirmed it for her. All of those things, they were true.

"Wow, that was a close call," Roger said, his eyes going wide at the thought of having to answer the little girl's questions.

"There, there," Beverly said, sighing, already thinking about the Sunday afternoon nap she was about to take.

CHAPTER NINE

Lizzie stared out the window. Still snowing. She got up out of bed and walked to the window. The traffic on the highway out at the edge of the field moved slowly through the heavy flakes, and Lizzie realized she wouldn't make it to Detroit, not in that kind of weather.

She felt both relieved and disappointed at the thought that she was more or less trapped at The Hope Center, at least for now. Her breath fogged up the glass, and she drew a small cross on the window with her finger. A crossroads. A decision point.

It was the quiet, really, that she found hard to deal with. And the slow pace. Before she got picked up off the street, her life was a series of sprints, from this job to the next, from this house to the next, get in a few hours of sleep and start it all over again. Life was a series of shouts and screams and arguments.

But at The Hope Center, all was quiet. She could literally hear the snow, when it was heavy, brushing against the window. She could hear girls in neighboring rooms laughing or crying or talking about their most recent counseling session. It was a difficult place for her to exist, in that peace and quiet, and she found herself resisting its gentle restraints.

She moved over to the small mirror and brushed her hair, over and over and over again, and as the brush ran through and released the knots, she closed her eyes. She pictured the snow falling. She remembered the church service on Sunday. She remembered Jane's words at her last session:

I think you're ready to join our group sessions, Lizzie. Come down to the meeting room tomorrow morning at nine.

Lizzie put her brush down on the small dresser and stared at the clock. 8:57. She sighed, took one last glance out the window, then walked out her door, turned right and made the long walk to the room at the end of the hall.

"Good morning, everyone," Jane said from the middle of the table. The room they sat in had a high, white ceiling made up of those square tiles, dark wood paneling on the walls, and a sort of green carpet that was faded in spots and flattened by years of conversation. The table they all sat around was an almost black wood covered with scratches and gouges. It was soft, so soft that even a fingernail could leave a mark.

"Good morning," some of the other girls mumbled. Only Penny said "Good morning" loudly, and after everyone else had spoken. This brought a chorus of giggles from the girls.

"Good morning, Penny," Jane said, smiling.

Then she turned to see a very young looking woman sitting to her right. The girl had stylish hair and bright makeup. Her nails were done and she held her pen and yellow lined notepad in front of her like a shield. Her eyes were large and nervous.

"This is Dawn," Jane said. "She's an intern from ECU majoring in social work, and she'll be helping us here at The

Hope Center for the next few months. Can everyone please say hello to Dawn?"

A few random, mostly mumbled "hellos" rustled through the room.

"Hi," Dawn said in a quiet voice. "Thanks."

"Would you like to say anything to the women?" Jane asked Dawn.

"Um, sure, um, well, I'm like really, really happy to be here. I really love this house and I can't wait to get to know you all better. I'm just, well, I guess that's it, for now."

Lizzie had to smile.

I'm almost as nervous as she is, Lizzie thought, smiling to herself. But her smile turned to panic when she heard her own name spoken.

"And this is Lizzie," Jane said. "Most of you know her by now. She's going to be joining our group sessions from now on."

"Yay!" Penny said, and everyone laughed. Lizzie smiled, glad that Penny had broken the tension.

"Whenever someone new joins the group," Jane said, "I like to remind all of us why we're here, in this particular setting. We want to focus on allowing each of you to talk about how you're feeling here at The Hope Center. We also want to hear about your life before you arrived here, and what you look forward to about life after The Hope Center."

Jane paused and looked around the table.

"Most of all, this is a place for each of you to encourage one another. I get to speak with you one on one, so this isn't necessarily the place for me to do all the talking. Ideally, each of you would be the encouragers here, in this space. I want you to feel free to give honest, kind feedback to one another."

Jane looked at Dawn and smiled, shuffled through her notes.

"Oh, yes, and of course the most important part is that you each feel free to share things that you might be uncomfortable sharing elsewhere. I promise you that no one here will be shocked or offended by anything that you share. This is a safe place. You will not be judged or made fun of."

Everyone was quiet. Lizzie stared hard at the table in front of her. She couldn't imagine sharing anything with these girls. They were practically strangers. If they knew the things she had done, or the things that had been done to her, they would never look at her again. She imagined admitting to them that she was waiting for the first opportunity to run away – that would only get her into trouble. Why would she share any of those things?

"I think you'll be surprised at how good you feel after you share," Jane said, as if trying to answer Lizzie's unspoken question. "So let's get started."

She waited quietly. Lizzie felt like the spotlight was on her. Was she expected to talk since she was the new girl? Then a small, weak voice spoke up from the other end of the table.

"I'd like to go first, if that's okay Miss Jane."

It was Lori, the girl from Jacksonville who had somehow ended up in an Atlanta jail cell.

"Please, Lori, go ahead."

Lizzie stared over at the girl. Lori fidgeted with her fingers on the table, then put them down in her lap. She was a tiny girl, so mousy and small that the longer Lizzie looked at her, the younger she looked.

Why, she's probably younger than I am, Lizzie thought.

"There's a story that's been on my mind a lot this week, since our last meeting. Our last group meeting," she looked up at Jane, and Jane gave her a small nod of encouragement.

"Well, it's just that, with Christmas coming up, I guess I've been thinking a lot about Christmas," she said.

Lizzie hadn't even thought much about Christmas. Presents and carols and cookies, or at least that's what the movies had always said Christmas was about. For her, Christmas had always meant a few gifts from Nae, or a little extra money for makeup or drugs. What would Christmas mean now? What would Christmas mean here?

"I been thinking a lot about Christmas when I was a kid, before all this stuff happened to me, you know? And I remembered how when I was living with my grandma she used to take me to this old folks home. I was only, I don't know, maybe six, but she took me there and we'd walk around and sing Christmas songs to the old folks, just the two of us."

The other girls stared intently at Lori as she spoke. It was so still, it was almost as if no one was breathing.

"The funny thing is, neither one of us could sing, so we probably sounded terrible," she released the tiniest laugh, and the other girls echoed with their own laughs. "And my grandma, she always wanted to sing this one song and I didn't know all the words so I just kind of made them up as I went.

Everyone laughed again, Penny the loudest.

"That's it," Lori said. "That's what I been thinking about, this week."

"How do you feel when you remember singing those Christmas carols with your grandma?" Jane asked Lori.

Lori took a deep breath, then smiled, a simple, contented smile.

"I think it makes me feel love," she said slowly. "I think it makes me feel love, and I don't remember the last time I felt that way, until I was here."

The girl beside Lori reached over and took her hand. The girl on the other side patted her on the back.

"You get me every time," Penny complained, sniffing and wiping her eyes. Everyone laughed, but it was a different kind of laughter than before, filled with blessings and a sense of "I know what you're talking about." Jane let the moment hold, full of that gift of togetherness.

"Who else wants to share today?" she asked.

The girl beside Lori, the girl who had reached out and taken her hand (the girl who, in fact, still held Lori's hand), raised her other hand and looked around the group to see if anyone else was going to talk.

"Yes, Abigail?"

Abigail had dark black hair and brown eyes that seemed sad because they turned down at the outer edges. Even when she smiled, her sad eyes seemed to bring her face back to the middle.

"It's funny Lori would say that, 'cause I been thinking about Christmas, too. Maybe it's all the snow."

"Or maybe it's Jolene's cooking," Penny interrupted, and everyone laughed.

"Maybe," Abigail said, smiling softly through her sad eyes. "Maybe that's it. Homemade holiday goodies are the best."

She stopped for a minute, trying to regain her train of thought.

"So what does Christmas and the snow make you think about, Abigail?"

"Oh, yeah, so anyway I was thinking about Christmas, just like Lori, and I remembered my most favorite gift of all time. My momma came in one Christmas morning and to be honest I didn't think I was getting any presents. I hadn't been very good that year and I knew that we didn't have much money. But momma came in carrying a box wrapped in green paper, with small red Christmas trees. It was the most beautiful wrapping paper I'd ever seen, and I didn't even want to open the gift, that paper was so precious."

Abigail took a deep breath and Lori squeezed her hand.

"So I opened it real careful, I didn't even tear the paper. It was the most beautiful little doll, and I was so shocked that I didn't even take it out of the box. I just sat there staring at her."

Everyone waited. Lizzie realized she was holding her breath. There was such power in these stories.

"She had pink cheeks and ponytails. Her little lips had a space to put a bottle in."

A few of the girls nodded. They had similar memories.

"But I still didn't move. I just stared at her. I was so amazed," she said, trying to explain herself. "Then, I guess my momma didn't think I liked the gift so she started screaming at me about how hard she had to work for that doll and she picked up the box and threw it against the wall and took that beautiful green wrapping paper and crumpled it up into a huge ball. Then she left and slammed the door and locked it from the outside. Sometimes she locked me in my room - I wasn't always a very good girl."

Abigail added that last sentence as if she was trying to explain her mother's actions away, as if they were expected, as if it was appropriate for her mother to lock her in her room.

"But that was my favorite Christmas ever. I sat there and I flattened out the wrapping paper and I hid it in the bottom of my closet. Then I played with that doll all day. She was so beautiful."

"That wasn't okay," Penny erupted. "That wasn't okay, what your momma did."

The other girls murmured their disapproval.

"But it was a nice gift," Lori whispered. "A very nice gift."

"That's okay," Abigail said. "That's okay. 'Cause the whole thing got me thinking, especially Sunday at the end of the service when pastor up there was talking about Jesus and how he was a gift to us, and I thought about that doll my momma gave me. I realized what a beautiful gift Jesus is, and I thought, 'Why, I'd like to have that gift.'"

She stopped. Miss Jane nodded, encouraging her to continue.

"So that's why I walked up to the front after service. I guess I accepted that gift on Sunday. I accepted Jesus into my heart. I'm not sure what all that means just yet, but somehow I sense something new and wonderful deep inside of me."

Silence.

"What a nice gift," Lori said again, and all the girls knew she wasn't talking about the doll.

Lizzie loved the story, at least until the end. The part about going up front in a church and talking to God made her uncomfortable. When Lori said "What a nice gift," Lizzie sort of laughed a quick, almost-silent laugh through her nose and leaned back in her chair, crossing her arms.

Jane looked over at Lizzie.

"Is there something you would like to say, Lizzie?" she asked.

"Churches don't give good gifts," she said quietly.

"I'm sorry, I don't think everyone could hear you," Jane said.

"I said, Churches don't give good gifts."

A few of the other girls looked down at the table, avoiding the conflict. Lori and Abigail let go of each other's hands and stared at Lizzie, waiting.

"I'm sorry," she said to Abigail, apologetic, "I loved the gift your momma gave you. That was nice. Real nice. But I know about churches, and they can't give good gifts. I know."

"Why do you say that, Lizzie?" Jane tried to draw Lizzie out.

But Lizzie had regained control of herself, and she stared quietly at the table, her hands moving to the sides of her chair.

Lori broke the silence.

"She didn't say the church gave her a gift, Lizzie! She's talking about God! God gave her the gift of Jesus! You'd understand that if you didn't have such a bad attitude toward church!"

"God?" Lizzie erupted. "God? Ha!"

"Ladies," Ms. Jane interjected in her typical calm and reassuring voice, "I need to remind you that even if we disagree with what is being shared, we need to speak with kindness and consideration of each other. This is not a place of judgment or criticism."

Lizzie moved uncomfortably in her chair and leaned forward, then back again, pushing away her bangs with her hands. It was a harsh movement, trying not to spill her anger.

"If God exists, and if you ask me that's a big if, then there isn't one of us, not one of us," and Lizzie looked around the table before continuing, "that's good enough for the gift you are talking about. Think about what we've done!"

She stopped and stared at a deep gash in the table. Images rushed through her mind, images of men and dark rooms and pain and drugs to numb it.

"The God in the pages of the Bible doesn't overlook your mistakes," she whispered. "It's called sin."

Her voice almost sounded like a plea for help.

"I think about all that filth and all those places and all those men, and I think, even if there was a God, there's no way I'm good enough. No way. I wasn't good enough for him to rescue me *then*, and I'm not good enough for him to rescue me *now*!"

Lizzie trembled, and she hugged her arms around herself. A few of the other girls cried without moving, tears streaming down their faces, leaving shining trails on their cheeks. Jane didn't interrupt the silence. She let the moment linger. Finally, an unfamiliar voice broke the silence.

"Lizzie," someone said, and she had to look up because she didn't recognize the voice at first. It was the intern, Dawn, the tiny girl sitting across from Jane. Before continuing, Dawn looked to Jane for permission to speak. Jane nodded her approval.

"I'm really, really glad you said that because it reminded me of something my dad always used to say."

The word 'dad' caught in Lizzie's mind. Even after so many years, she couldn't understand people who talked about their dads as though it was natural, as though everyone in the world had a dad. She stared at Dawn, waiting for her to continue.

"So my dad used to say this about God all the time. He'd say, 'Good people don't go to Heaven. You have to be perfect.' And the first time he said that I was pretty young and it shocked me. I was like, 'But dad, that's impossible. No one's perfect.' And he was like, 'Dawn, that's the point. You have to be perfect, but you're not, and that's why Jesus came to die, because the blood he shed on the cross can make you perfect.'"

Every girl in the room listened then. There were no windows, but Lizzie thought she could hear the snow sliding over the roof of the house.

Dawn continued, softly but confidently, "You're right Lizzie, God can't overlook our sin because he is perfect. His Heaven is also perfect. There is no need for locks on the doors, There is no need for police in Heaven. There is no crime, no wrong and no harm in Heaven because Heaven is only populated by a perfect God and his perfect people."

Dawn paused, wondering if she was overstepping her boundaries as a new co-leader. Every girl sat silent, hanging on Dawn's last words.

Jane gently interjected, "Please continue Dawn. It's alright."

Dawn swallowed hard understanding the gravity of

moment. She dabbed a tear from the corner of her eye, gave a reassuring smile and then leaned in towards the group.

"Lizzie understands that sin is a big deal to God. Sin stains us. Sin contaminates us. And I'm not just talking about the people in this room. By the time everyone reaches their teen years, they've all experienced shame over a wrong choice or felt guilt over doing something wrong. Sin always happens, because not one of us is perfect."

She thought for a moment. One of the girls passed a box of Kleenex around the table.

"No one has to teach a child how to be selfish or how to lie or how to be mean to a little sister," Dawn said. "Sin naturally flows out of our imperfection as humans. Sometimes people think that being good can make up for sin, but it doesn't. We're still stained, imperfect and in need of perfection. It's bad...real bad."

Dawn made sure to make eye contact with every girl in the group, but she was especially aware of Lizzie's gaze that was fixed on her.

"But in all this badness, God brings us good news, the good news of Jesus. Somehow, God made a way for us to be forgiven and cleansed from our sin through Jesus' death on the cross. And more than this, when we accept the gift of Jesus, the Bible tells us that the old imperfect person is cut away from the inside and we become a new person in Christ. Even though we may look the same on the outside and even though we may struggle with some of the same negative thoughts and poor behavior, on the inside we are changed. God makes us perfect and then he begins to slowly change us from the inside out. Day by day, as we learn to live by faith in God and what God has done, our perfection becomes more and more noticeable. First in the way we think and then in the way we live."

Without warning Abigail exclaimed, "Yes! That's exactly

what the pastor said! That's what I did last Sunday. I admitted my sin to God, asked for forgiveness and accepted Jesus as my perfection."

Lizzie dropped her eyes away from Dawn's gaze. Her finger followed a long, crooked scratch mark on the table and she wondered, for an instant, who had made that scratch. How long ago? What had they been doing? What had they been talking about?

The scratch disappeared under her Bible. And there, peeking out from between the pages was the bookmark Jane had given her. Her eyes locked in on one of the statements of truth:

In Christ, I am redeemed and forgiven.

She went back to her room and wrote in her journal.

"A New Identity in Christ" Wednesday, 9:18pm

Today was hard. I am so tired of feeling angry. I am so tired of hurting others with my words. I am so tired of feeling like I need to bully others so that they won't see my weakness. Why do I always try to be the tough girl?

Miss Jane and Miss Jolene sure have a lot of patience with me. They say that my mind needs to accept the truth that I can have a brand new identity in Christ. I still don't understand what they mean. Even though I am still Lizzie, I would no longer be Lizzie the foster kid, Lizzie the runaway, Lizzie the prostitute. Instead, in Christ, I become all these things on this silly bookmark. Lizzie a saint? That makes me laugh just to write that. I sure didn't sound like a saint when I yelled at Lori today. I am mean by nature. Is God big enough to change me?

God... if you are listening, you need to know that I have my doubts about you. You might be as wonderful as some of these people claim, but I don't think you care much about me. Maybe it's because I'm just bad to the core. Maybe you choose your favorites and I'm not on that list.

But maybe it's possible that I've never really understood you. Maybe I've been wrong all these years. So here is your chance. If you are real, I need to know. If you are good, I need to understand. If you can love me, I have to know how. Help me to see you. Help me to see you in my past, my present, and my future.

CHAPTER TEN

The day that Matthew Blair's brother Mark waited for Lizzie in the janitor's closet was a hot day. Lizzie would always remember that it was in the summer because she was hot and sweaty and tired of all those people at the church, even those who looked at her with pity in their eyes. Perhaps especially tired of those people. She was so tired.

She didn't sleep well at night. She had no friends except for Jennifer from her Sunday School class, and Jennifer's parents were skeptical about letting Elizabeth play with Jennifer too much. So it was a stagnant friendship, one that never grew. Elizabeth would lie there at night staring at the ceiling and when she finally fell asleep she dreamed about having friends who waited for her at school, or having a dad who protected her from anyone who wanted to harm her.

On that hot summer day the church basement was full of people and their voices. It was some kind of festival or church-wide picnic and everyone was down in the basement or walking out the back doors to the long yard that sloped down towards a narrow stream. Whenever someone opened the doors, heat rushed in. It was an overwhelming heat, the kind that made elderly people sit down, the kind of heat that made little children sweat until they looked like they had been baptized.

Someone thought it would be a good idea to connect the hose and some of the older children sprayed some of the younger children as they shrieked and ran in the slippery grass. Lizzie lost track of Roger and Beverly and her two brothers. She stood quietly on the fringe of everything, waiting. She wasn't dressed for getting wet, and she didn't have any clothes to change into.

Jennifer wasn't there that day, or perhaps none of it ever would have happened. None of it. If only Jennifer had been there that day! But she wasn't, and there was no one else to take her place.

One of the older children saw Elizabeth standing there on the fringe and sprayed her with a hose. It was a harmless thing to do, perhaps even a kind thing, an attempt to draw Elizabeth into the fun, but it was not what Elizabeth wanted. Immediately she was soaked through, her dress clinging to her skin, and it embarrassed her. She didn't want to be wet around all those people. She didn't want her dress to stick to her like that.

So she ran inside and the cold air made her wet dress feel like an icy wrapping around her. She weaved in and out among the adults who stood in small groups holding their iced tea and laughing. They didn't even see her as she slipped past, as she moved into the stairway and then moved like a shadow into the janitor's closet.

Elizabeth could breathe in there. It gave her a sense of space and the much-needed time to gather herself, to think. She held on to the door knob for a moment, surrounded by complete darkness, and it felt like things would be okay. But it would not be okay, not for a long time.

She flipped on the small overhead light. Nothing happened.

"It's better that way," she mumbled quietly to herself.

There was something peaceful in the darkness, something she was happy to sit in. She searched in the dark and found an old five-gallon bucket, flipped it upside-down, then sat on it. She hugged her arms tightly around herself, trying to find some warmth, and it wasn't as cold there in the closet, but she still felt chilled.

She thought about her life. She thought about Sunday School and Mr. Sanders and Roger and Beverly. The memories she had of the trailer where she had lived with her mom were fading as she grew older. After only a few years she found certain things difficult to picture, and it frustrated her. Like the kitchen – what had their kitchen looked like? She remembered the couch and the television and the hallway. But what about the bathroom? She couldn't remember the bathroom.

She wished she knew where her mother had gone and what had happened to her. She wished someone would be honest with her.

She wondered what had happened to that kind social worker, Kate somebody. She couldn't remember her last name. She wished she would show up right there at the church and rescue her again, take her to a new home. Of all the foster homes she had been to, why had Roger and Beverly "stuck"? Why couldn't they tire of her like everyone else had? She wanted to move on. This wasn't working.

And always, somewhere in the back of her mind, were questions about her father. She knew he wasn't like Roger, quiet and imposing. She knew her father wouldn't have been like Mr. Sanders or any other man she had ever met. She thought her father must be very kind and would always keep her by his side at times like this, when there were too many other adults around. He wouldn't leave her standing on the edge of the circle, and if a child sprayed her with a hose he would step in and tell that child how it was. He'd pick her up and take her to the car, drive her home and get her a fresh set of clothes. Then they'd watch television together or (better yet) go get ice cream.

Elizabeth started to cry there in the darkness as she contemplated who she wanted her father to be, what she wanted him to be like. She cried because she didn't have a father like that, and she cried because she didn't have any true friends, and she cried because she hated living with Roger and Beverly. But mostly she cried because, somewhere deep inside, she knew that her father was not kind or protective or loving because if he had been he never would have left her.

Then she felt a hand on her shoulder, and she screamed and stood up.

"Sh! It's okay," a voice said, and she knew it was Mark Blair. The older boy's voice was caught in between boyhood and manhood, and she recognized it immediately. She also knew that, no matter what he said, things were definitely not okay.

He didn't move his hand from her shoulder. His fingers felt warm against her cold, wet dress and they held tight, like talons.

"What are you crying about?" he asked.

Again she was aware of the darkness in the closet, but now it pressed against her, wrapped around her. She couldn't breathe. She had to fight just to whisper.

"Nothing," she said.

"C'mon! You must be crying about something."

She shook her head, but he couldn't have seen that in the

darkness. Maybe he felt her body move slightly.

"It's okay. You don't have to tell me."

And still his hand was on her shoulder. She became intensely aware of the smells in the room: cleaning supplies combined with wet mops and dusty brooms. She caught the hint of cologne, something Mark must have been wearing, and she couldn't believe she didn't notice it before. She couldn't believe she hadn't smelled it as soon as she entered the closet. She should have smelled it. She should have run right back out.

He moved closer. She knew, not because she could see him move, not because she felt him move, but because she heard the slight scuffling of his feet on the concrete floor. Then she felt his other hand on her other shoulder.

"It's going to be okay," he whispered, and she was so scared and so shocked that she couldn't move. Inside her head she screamed, "Run! Run!" but her body wouldn't listen.

When she darted through the door five minutes later, the darkness of that janitor's closet had lodged permanently inside her. It had gone from being an abstract thing that surrounded her to a physical pain, a heavy knot in the pit of her stomach. She knew she wouldn't ever be the same. She felt dirty and unworthy. All she wanted to do was go home and take a bath, but somehow she knew that even the hottest water couldn't change what had just happened, couldn't take her back to who she had been before.

She ran up the stairs and through the foyer and into the parking lot. She found Roger and Beverly's car and got in and waited for them. She didn't ever want to go back to that church, but she knew she'd have to go back the next Sunday and the next and the next. She remembered all of the Sunday School lessons about a righteous God, a God who demanded perfection.

Elizabeth thought, in that moment, that there was never anything she could do to make this up to God. She was sure that she was beyond saving.

This is when she began to consider running away from Roger and Beverly – not just as some kind of pipe dream, but as a reality. She began to plan the more practical aspects, like where she would go and what she would take with her.

When Roger and Beverly came out to the car with the boys, they were not happy.

"Where were you, young lady? We looked everywhere for you!" Beverly said from the passenger seat as the car pulled out of the church parking lot. Her voice was stern, and Elizabeth could also tell she was embarrassed. She had probably been forced to ask other people to help her find Elizabeth.

"Mom!" one of the boys complained. "She's all wet! She's getting me all wet!"

"When we get home," Roger said quietly, "you will come back out to the car and dry off the seat."

"We were worried about you!" Beverly protested. "We didn't know where you had gone! Something terrible could have happened to you!"

But Elizabeth didn't say anything. She sat there quietly, pulled her dress closer so that the boys would stop complaining, and tried to figure out what she could do with that darkness inside her.

CHAPTER ELEVEN

"Let's go, girls," Jolene shouted as she waddled down the hallway. "Surprise trip today!"

Lizzie heard some of the girls moan from their rooms. It was cold outside, and the snow on the roads and the sidewalks had turned into a thick slush that soaked everyone to the bone. It wasn't snowing anymore, but a harsh winter wind battered the windows. The girls were content to spend their free time in the house, preferably in their rooms, under a warm blanket.

"Aw, Jolene," Lizzie heard Penny protest from the kitchen. "It's freezing out there."

"Surprise trip, surprise trip," Jolene responded in a sing-song voice. The girls slowly put on their layers of warm clothes, most of them donated from a local thrift store, and stood in the small entryway waiting until everyone was ready. All the layers of clothes turned them into formless eskimos, and few of the articles matched. As they walked outside, they became a colorful parade in the white snow.

Lizzie didn't mind. She was always happy to leave the

house, mostly because she had never been much of a homebody. She always preferred going out to staying in. But there was another reason she was eager to go out. She had decided that she was definitely going to do it.

She was definitely going to run away.

She pulled a knit hat on her head and thought about it. She still didn't have much of a plan. She'd need a little money – not much – and she thought she could smuggle some food from the kitchen. She didn't think transportation would be an issue, since they were so close to the highway, and she knew she needed to get out of the area fast. They'd be looking for her.

"Let's go, let's go," Jolene said as they walked through the cold day, and then she giggled. "You're all gonna love this."

They piled into the van, squeezed together even tighter than usual because of their puffy clothing. The girls in the back chatted and called to the ones in the front. Everyone was in a festive mood, now that they were out and in a van that was warming up. The heat blasted from the vents, and Lizzie pulled the knit hat off her head, growing drowsy in the warmth.

"Where are we going?" the girls kept asking, but Jolene just smiled and made a motion with one of her hands across her mouth, as if she was zipping her lips closed.

As they drove, Lizzie thought about the group session from a few nights before. She thought back through Dawn's talk, her thoughts on God and Jesus and perfection. There was a small spark deep inside Lizzie that wanted to believe it all, but to be honest it seemed too good to be true. Too simple.

You can't just erase everything bad you've ever done by saying a few words, she thought.

The day was bright and they drove past a school, the teacher's cars parked in the front parking lot. The playground was empty and cold, covered in ice and snow and waiting for spring. The wind whipped the flag into a frenzy. Lizzie stared at the slide and the swings, the jungle gym and the monkey bars.

Soon the van turned into the church parking lot, the same church they had all attended on Sunday, and parked by the front entrance. Lizzie sighed. She was tired of church. She was tired of all the memories it brought back, painful memories, things she'd rather bury in her mind. Even though she was in the front of the van, she was the last to get out. She trailed far behind the others. By the time she got around the van, the front doors of the church had closed and she had to open them for herself.

She walked into the warm lobby. That's when she saw the envelope almost completely hidden under one of the inside doors that was propped open. She looked around. Everyone had already gone into the sanctuary. She reached down and pulled the envelope out from under the door. It had the word "Offering" on it. There was something inside, but she couldn't tell what it was because the envelope was sealed. She thought about tearing it open right there, on the spot.

"Lizzie?" Jolene called from inside the sanctuary. "Where's Lizzie?"

That lady is like a hawk, Lizzie thought to herself. *How will I ever escape with her always on the lookout?*

"Coming!" Lizzie shouted, tucking the envelope into her coat pocket without opening it. She'd have to wait until they got back to the house, but she had a good feeling about it. A very good feeling.

"So," Jolene said. "This is it!"

She beckoned towards a massive evergreen tree at the front right of the church's auditorium, waving towards it with both hands like a game show host showing off a prize. The tree smelled wonderful, like some kind of Christmas candle.

The girls stared at her, waiting for more information.

"It's a Christmas Tree!" Jolene said.

"We know that," Penny said in an annoyed voice. "We're not that stupid."

"Oh, Penny," Jolene said, waving her hand at the girl. "Stop that. It's a Christmas Tree...that we get to decorate!"

Some of the girls smiled. Some of them didn't look too excited. Lizzie was shocked – the days had gotten away from her.

"It's almost Christmas?" she asked.

"Yes, it's almost Christmas," Jolene said.

"What's the date?" Lizzie asked.

"Christmas is next Sunday," Jolene said.

Panic rose inside Lizzie. Next Sunday? That meant Nae and the girls would probably be moving soon. They always moved at the end of the year. Nae got nervous and thought people were tracking them down, so he always made a point of finding some other place for them to stay.

If she didn't get back to Detroit soon, she didn't know if she'd be able to find him again. She thought of the endless streets of that city, the abandoned buildings and the bustling areas full of people that spilled out into the suburbs. The sprawling apartment buildings and tenement houses. She suddenly felt adrift in the world, as if the line attaching her to an anchor had been cut. It was all she could do to keep from turning around and sprinting to the highway.

The other girls had all walked forward to the stage where a line of boxes waited for them. Each box held a different kind of decoration: strands of silver tinsel, ropes and ropes of beads, detailed ornaments, white lights and red lights and green lights. Soon they were all chattering about what they were finding, and, as usual, Penny's voice rose up above the rest.

"Okay, okay," she said. "Now you always start with the

lights. That way the rest of the stuff hides all the cords."

So a few of them began untangling strands of lights while a few others found the extension cords and some outlets backstage, but they didn't plug anything in yet – that should be saved for last, Penny told them. They walked around and around the tree, and they had to use a ladder once they got to the upper parts. Jolene just stood off to the side, swaying back and forth to some song in her head, smiling.

Lizzie picked a small ornament out of one of the boxes. It was a miniature snow globe with a hook on it so that it could be fastened to the tree. Inside the globe was a tiny, bustling city. Miniature cars were on the streets and people the size of ants walked the sidewalks. The buildings stretched up high on either side of the street, and she could tell it was Christmas in that tiny place because there were wreaths hanging from the streetlights and a Christmas tree in the city square.

She turned it upside down, then right side up. The snow swirled around the skyscrapers and the cars and the people. She shook it a little to keep the snow moving, and she sighed. She reached down and felt the envelope in her pocket, and even though she didn't know what was inside it, something about it made her feel better.

It took about an hour to decorate the tree, and the girls started putting the leftover decorations back in the box. Abigail was crying and smiling at the same time, and Lori went over and put her arm around her. But Lizzie stood back, watching, holding the snow globe.

"The star!" Penny shouted. "The star! Who's going to put the star on the tree?"

After much discussion, someone shouted out.

"You do it, Penny! You're the star of Atlanta!"

Everyone laughed.

"Well," Penny said, "I think I'm the queen of Atlanta, but

today I can be the star if you want."

They laughed again. Even Lizzie smiled.

Penny climbed slowly up the ladder and it shook so a few of the girls steadied it for her. She reached nervously over to the topmost point of the evergreen tree and perched the star on top, then plugged it in to the end of the lights. She climbed down.

"Now," Jolene said. "The church has said that you can each pick out one ornament to take with you, if you'd like."

The girls cheered a miniature cheer and scrambled through the boxes. Some walked back up to the tree and took down something that had caught their eye while they had been decorating. Lizzie clutched the miniature snow globe in her hand.

"Aren't you going to choose one, Lizzie?" Jolene asked her.

Lizzie held up the miniature snow globe.

"I was already looking at this one," she said. "I think I'll hang on to it."

Jolene smiled and nodded, then turned to face the rest of the girls who were talking and showing each other what they had chosen.

"Finally," Jolene said. "One last thing. Penny, go back and get ready to plug in the tree. But first let me go turn off the lights."

Penny dashed backstage while Jolene headed back up the center aisle, swaying back and forth as she walked. It was a long, slow journey. Finally she turned off the auditorium lights, and all that Lizzie could see was the bright glare through the doors of the outside world, blinding and white. She couldn't see Jolene come back down the aisle but she could hear her. She was humming a Christmas tune.

"Okay," Jolene called out to Penny. "Plug it in!"

"I can't see!" she shouted, and all the girls laughed, but then she must have found the outlet because the tree lit up, and it took the girls' breath away. The bright white lights shone like stars, and the tinsel reflected the light, looked like strands of silver.

And the star on top? It was glorious. For the first time in a long time, Lizzie remembered the story behind Christmas. She imagined Mary and Joseph and their little baby huddled in a stable while a star shone high up in the sky.

They all stood there in silence. Lizzie sat down in one of the front row seats and stared at that glowing tree. She couldn't remember the last time she had seen something so beautiful that it made her ache.

I could sit here forever, she thought.

Back at The Hope Center, the girls walked into their rooms and changed into cooler clothing. There was a lightness to the way that everyone walked, an air of hope and possibility. Those moments of happiness, like decorating the tree, helped the girls to feel like they could move beyond their past.

All the girls, that is, except for Lizzie.

She couldn't shake her desire to run away. In fact, with each passing minute the desire grew stronger and stronger. It seemed like it was all she could think about: how she could get some money, steal some food, and hitch a ride to Detroit. How she could escape the eagle eyes of Jolene. What she would do when she got back there.

And now the clock was ticking because Nae would be changing locations soon. Maybe he already had. Maybe he already had! Maybe she'd never find him again.

She walked into her room and nudged the door behind her so that it drifted within three inches of being closed. She had five minutes until her weekly appointment with Jane. She sat on her bed and turned her back to the door. She reached into her pocket and pulled out the envelope, which by then had become wrinkled and torn at the corners from being stuffed into her pockets and from her hand which had constantly felt for it to make sure she hadn't lost it.

She stared at it for a minute. She knew an offering was money someone gave to God. She had been in church long enough to know that. Her fingernail snagged on to a loose edge at the corner of the envelope and she pulled, tearing it open.

Two twenty dollar bills. Forty dollars. It wasn't much, but it would help. She glanced over her shoulder, then walked to the window. A piece of trim was loose around the window sill, and she slid the folded bills into that space. She walked back over and sat down on the bed, staring at the window to see if someone could see the small paper edge sticking up. She didn't think they would.

She balled up the envelope and squeezed it in her fist, then walked out of her room and down the hall. She ignored Penny's greeting, ignored the other two girls she passed. She walked straight into the bathroom and locked the door, then put the balled-up envelope into the toilet. She waited. Waited. Then she flushed, and she watched the paper disappear.

Lizzie sighed. Then she walked back to her room, picked up her Bible with the bookmark in it, and walked upstairs for her session with Jane.

She was almost ready to leave. She could feel it.

CHAPTER TWELVE

The years crept by for Elizabeth. She turned eight, and that long year was like a century, with its own battles and losses and disappointments. Time always trudges along when you're not where you want to be.

Roger and Beverly had a small birthday party for her, a nice party, but it didn't match up to Elizabeth's memory of Justine's party when she was four years old. Probably because Elizabeth's real father never came bursting through the door, never picked her up and spun her around, never made her feel like a true daughter. For this reason, they weren't memorable. The gifts were meaningless, like the smoke that hung around the room after she blew out the candles.

"Did you enjoy your birthday?" Roger asked her every year.

"Yes, thank you," Elizabeth would say as she carried an armful of presents up to her room and gently closed the door.

Some things changed during that year. Mr. Sanders, for example, was no longer her teacher. When she turned eight she moved up to a different Sunday School class led by a mostly-kind woman whose name she could never remember. There were new children who came to class and some of the older children moved on. So, in that way, things were not always the same.

Her two brothers grew older. As they did, they thought about her less and less, which was actually a blessing because this forgetfulness led to less teasing, less complaining. She preferred her new invisibility to the prior life of constant spats and conflicts.

Some things didn't change, the worst of which was Mark Blair. For more than a year he didn't leave her alone. It wasn't that she went back to the janitor's closet. In fact, she never went back inside that closet, not ever again. Each time she hurried by the door, she felt sick to her stomach and couldn't keep from blushing with embarrassment at what had happened inside.

She was still a girl on the run, a girl not understood very well by adults and overlooked by other children. She found different hiding places during that year, places she hoped Mark Blair would not think to look: under the back steps that went up a roundabout way to the stage in the main meeting room; in the dark kitchen that was rarely used on Sundays, except for special events; in an empty Sunday School room that didn't have any windows. Each new place, each new darkness, offered her hope that this would be the sanctuary she had always been looking for.

But everywhere she went, Mark found her. Not right away, because she was small and quick and good at hiding. But eventually all her places came undone. Once, she even considered going back to the janitor's closet – he would never expect that – but just putting her hand on the door knob gave her flashbacks to that first time. She ran the rest of the way up the stairs and stood in the lobby by herself for ten minutes, trembling, until the classes ended and everyone flooded the foyer.

Why didn't she stop hiding, if he always found her? Why didn't she just stay in class or go tell Roger and Beverly? Why? Because she couldn't stop hiding. It was a compulsion, a reaction, something in her nature. After all, she had so many things to hide from: her disappointment with her current family, loneliness, and, most of all, the darkness that had taken root inside her.

And she also hid for the same reason that anyone hides: because she wanted to be found. Not by Mark of course, but she wanted to know that she could run away, far away, and that someone loving and protective would come after her and pull her from the darkness. Someone who would search for her no matter how far or how fast she ran. Someone who would look until they found her.

But no one did that. No one besides Mark, and he wasn't there to love or protect her. He was there to use her and then leave.

And that's what he did, eventually: he left. She finally found relief. Mark went off to college, a Christian college far away and he rarely came home except during holidays. Eventually he didn't even come home for holidays or summers. The halls of the church held much less malice for Elizabeth, and her hiding places were quiet again and safe.

In some ways she finally felt free. Or at least that's how she thought she should feel. But even after Mark left, she realized it would take more than his absence to bring her freedom from all that he had done to her. Even at nine years old she knew it would take more than a lack of Mark to release her into a new life.

In fact, even after Mark went away to college, she soon realized that his presence was still there, haunting her. He had somehow become part of the darkness inside her, the darkness she couldn't get rid of. How badly she wanted to rid herself of it!

One thing she noticed after everything that Mark had done to her was that she now had a sense about men and boys, a sort of ability to tell if they were the kind of men or boys who, if given the chance, might do what Mark had done. It was difficult to explain, this feeling, but it usually had something to do with the way they looked at her or didn't look at her, the way they said certain things to her or didn't talk at all.

If she would have had friends back then she would have explained it by saying something like, "That guy? He gives me the creeps!" Then she and her friend would have pretended to throw up and they would have laughed and snubbed whoever it was that "gave them the creeps."

But she didn't have any friends, and she didn't have anyone to laugh with, so she began to think that when she "got the creeps" it was her own fault, that these particular men or boys made her feel that way because something was wrong with her, not them. She felt like something was broken inside of her.

One of these particular young men who gave her the creeps was Roger's nephew Steve. He had green eyes that were a little too large for his head, an almost constant leer on his face, and bad acne. He was around fourteen, tall for his age, and carried a comb in his jeans pocket that he used for all kinds of things besides brushing his hair. Things like flicking people or picking at his teeth.

When he looked at her, Steve gave Elizabeth the creeps.

Elizabeth's ninth birthday was a hastily arranged affair. It felt like Beverly had nearly forgotten about it, and it felt that way because that's what had almost happened. The two boys had sports and other activities that kept Beverly busy every

96

night of the week. Beverly was one of those women who believe that girls shouldn't play sports. She would never have said something like that out loud, but she also would never sign her own girl up for soccer or basketball.

"Sports are all rather, well, masculine. Don't you think?" she asked her friends when they went out to eat.

So while she drove the boys all over the county every night of the week for their next athletic practice or competition, Elizabeth's outlet was the piano. She didn't like the piano, and she liked it even less because it meant she was confined to the house for her practices. The piano teacher, a white-haired woman named Ethel, came three times a week for thirty minutes and tapped on her head with a white stick when she lost the rhythm. This was not Elizabeth's idea of a fun time, and she resented the boys even more because of their freedom.

In the midst this family chaos, Roger and Beverly nearly forgot about Elizabeth's birthday. It didn't help that her birthday was January 14, only a few weeks into the new year and during that time when everyone is still gasping for breath after the holidays. When they finally realized her birthday was a few days away, it was too late to bring together a proper gathering. Everyone Elizabeth knew had already made plans.

"It's fine," Beverly told Roger. "We'll just make it a family affair."

When Elizabeth found out the day before her party that it was going to be a "family affair," she wasn't all that disappointed – not until she heard that Steve and his family were coming over.

"What! Not Steve!" Elizabeth whined.

"What do you mean, 'Not Steve?'" Roger asked in a voice that implied Elizabeth should be thankful for the party and not so picky about who would be in attendance. "He's your cousin, and his father is my favorite brother."

He stared at her for a moment to make sure she knew how upset he was then walked away, still mumbling to himself.

"What does she mean by 'Not Steve'?"

But in the end, Beverly managed to invite a few of the children from Elizabeth's Sunday School class, too. Elizabeth sighed. She had become used to the disappointment that always accompanied her birthdays, and she already wished it was over. She was turning nine, but she wished she was turning 18 or 21 or 30. When she thought of how many birthdays remained between her and the ability to leave Roger and Beverly, it made her feel trapped and overwhelmed.

Elizabeth was blindfolded, and she swung the stick. The crowd groaned when she missed and erupted in a cheer when the stick made contact. She veered from side to side in the darkness and almost lost her balance when she swung and missed.

She swung again and the stick finally broke through. She heard the screams of the children and the shouts of the adults as they all converged on the candy that had spilled into the center of the living room. She pulled back the blindfold and stared at the broken piñata, still dangling from a makeshift rope that Roger had somehow rigged to an old light fixture.

"Elizabeth? Elizabeth!" Beverly shouted. "Get some candy before it's all taken."

She bent over and picked up a few pieces of bubble gum, a few lollipops. Then she put them in a paper bag that she had written her name on.

Elizabeth.

The letters were crooked and wavering, like the letters advertising a Halloween event. It had been difficult to write on the bag, especially while standing up. But that was her name.

Elizabeth.

She picked up a few more pieces of candy and put them in the bag, then followed the children as they raced into the kitchen to eat their candy and get ready for the cake. Just in front of her was a boy from her Sunday School class. His name was Phil Tucker and she thought he was just about the cutest boy she had ever seen in her life.

As they walked towards the kitchen she heard him complain to her cousin Steve that he hadn't picked up any bubblegum.

It took immense courage, but she tapped him on the shoulder. He turned, and he seemed surprised to see her there.

"I have some bubble gum, plenty of it," she said. She couldn't believe the words were coming out. She couldn't believe she was talking to Phil Tucker. And just like that, they stopped. Whatever it was in her brain that made the words, it stopped working, so she reached into her bag and pulled out a few pieces, held them towards Phil Tucker.

But his surprise turned to disgust and he didn't reach for the gum. Instead he leaned in close and whispered.

"I don't want your gum. I don't even want to be here – my mom made me come."

The blood drained from her face. She wanted to cry, or run away, but he kept whispering. He wouldn't stop whispering.

"I know about Mark," he said, shaking his head, almost in disbelief. "I know what you did with him."

Then it was almost as if the disgust overwhelmed him to the point where he couldn't talk to her anymore. He turned and walked into the kitchen, leaving her in the hall with Steve.

She could tell that Steve hadn't heard everything that Phil had said. He put his hand on her shoulder and tried to give her a nice smile, but it still came out crooked and leering.

"It's okay, Lizzie," he said, and the feel of his hand on her shoulder made her tremble. "Don't worry about him."

But she wasn't worried about Phil. She was worried about

Steve. And she hated when people called her Lizzie.

"Elizabeth," Beverly called from the kitchen. "Are you coming, or what? Everyone's waiting for you!"

Elizabeth walked into the kitchen and everyone started singing "Happy Birthday to You!" The candles on the cake burned brightly but the darkness inside her grew. When the song finished, she leaned in and blew the candles out, and a cloud of smoke surrounded her. She wanted to hide in it.

CHAPTER THIRTEEN

An eruption of laughter came from the kitchen of The Hope Center, rippled down the hall and then moved in a wave past the empty dorm rooms and through the Saturday night air. It moved alongside the smell of baking Christmas cookies and the sound of Christmas music playing on the crackling stereo speakers in Jolene's room. In it was warmth and hope and a sense of togetherness that many of the girls had never felt before.

But one dorm room wasn't empty. Lizzie sat on her bed, thinking, planning, and wondering. A bedside lamp was on, the glare from it shining against the window that looked out on a dark night. Frost had already begun to form around the edges of the windows, and it was a clear night, a moonless night. Lizzie stared through the dark window as if the space beyond contained the answers to all of her questions.

Where was Nae at that exact moment, two days before Christmas? How would she get to Detroit before New Year's Day? What would be waiting for her when she arrived?

Lizzie pulled her journal out from under the mattress and leafed through the pages she had written. She went past the endless doodles and mazes she had drawn, then stopped at the first blank page she could find.

"God Owns Me?" Saturday, 7:20pm

Yesterday Miss Jane challenged me on my refusal to follow some of the minor rules of the house, things like leaving my door open or making sure to sweep off the front porch when it's on my chore list. She claimed I have "lingering rebellion" issues, whatever that means. She gave me this verse to write here in my journal and also told me to write what came to mind.

"Do you not know that your bodies are temples of the Holy Spirit, who is in you, whom you have received from God? You are not your own; you were bought at a price. Therefore honor God with your bodies." (1 Corinthians 6:19-20)

It's strange to think that I am not my own. I mean, it's strange and yet it's not, because of Nae. I don't know. That gets complicated.

But to think that God owns me. I think this gets back to what Miss Jane has been saying about not letting sin be my master. Do I want to live "free", do what I want, and then live in pain? Or would I rather have a master who keeps me safe, gives me what I need, and treats me with kindness?

The answer seems obvious – I always wanted Nae to be my master, to treat me with kindness. But he didn't do that. Could I trust someone enough to give them control of my life? I don't know.

"Lizzie?" a soft voice said at the door, followed by a few soft knocks on the hard wooden door. "You in there, girl?"

Lizzie sighed.

"Yep, I'm here."

A girl walked in, her cheeks flushed from the warmth of the kitchen. She carried a cookie in each hand and reached out to offer one to Lizzie.

"Thanks, Penny," Lizzie said. The small act of kindness brought tears to her eyes.

"What are you doing in here, girl?" she asked. "There's all kinds of goodness going on in that kitchen. This ain't a night for sittin' all alone."

Lizzie smiled.

"I'm just thinking, you know? Just thinking."

"Well, it's not a night for that, either," Penny said, and the girls both laughed.

"Penny, can I ask you something?"

Penny didn't say anything, but she walked around and sat at the foot of her bed. She stared at Lizzie. Lizzie drew her legs up to her chest and hugged them tight. She dropped her chin to one of her knees and when she spoke her words came out firm and unwavering.

"Why'd you stay?"

"Stay where?" Penny asked.

"Stay here," Lizzie said, looking up at Penny with such seriousness. It was as if the answer to that one question would determine everything. "Why'd you stay here?"

Penny looked off to the side for a moment, combing her recent history for the answer. Her thin face suddenly seemed older and tired, and Lizzie wished she could take back the question.

"Girl, I didn't have nothin' to go back to. Nothin'. Oh, there was men here and men there, and I guess I had a few girls I coulda called friends, some kind of friends anyway. So at first that's why I stayed - because I didn't have nothin' else."

Lizzie nodded, and Penny paused for a moment before continuing.

"But then, after a few months, things started movin' around in my head, things I didn't understand. New questions, questions I didn't ever ask before. So now I don't stay because I got nothin' else - now I stay because I have hope."

"Hope," Lizzie said, as if tasting some new kind of delicious fruit for the first time, but the kind of fruit she thought she might never taste again.

"Hope," Penny said, shrugging. "My friends, I don't know if they were friends, but they'd be saying right about now that 'Penny found Jesus,' and they'd laugh and laugh and make fun of me, I'm sure. But I guess they'd be right. What they don't understand is that I didn't just find Jesus. I mean, it was just him, but he gives me so much, you know?"

Lizzie shook her head.

"No, Penny, I honestly don't know."

"Oh, girl," Penny said, moving closer to Lizzie. "He gives me that hope. And a fresh start. And freedom. Most important, was that. Freedom."

Penny reached out and took one of Lizzie's hands, and the two girls sat there without saying anything. Time passed, and another wave of laughter rolled out of the kitchen. Lizzie lifted the cookie to her mouth and took a bite.

"So what's going on in the kitchen?" she asked.

Penny stood up.

"Why don't you come with me and find out for yourself?"

Lizzie smiled.

"Okay," she said. "These cookies are pretty good."

"Pretty good?" Penny asked in a shocked voice. "Pretty good? You call that cookie 'Pretty Good' anywhere within Miss Jolene's hearing and she'll swat you with the spatula."

Both girls laughed, and Penny leaned in close.

"Which wouldn't be totally bad," she whispered. "Because that cookie dough? Better than the cookies."

Both girls laughed again and walked into the warmth of the kitchen.

The next night, Sunday night, was Christmas Eve. Lights hung on the trees and it was a clear night so the entire town glowed. Cars made their way to the church and people, bundled in their warmest winter clothes, rushed inside, shaking off the cold and smiling at one another. A young woman read the Christmas story in a clear voice in front of the black stage curtain, lit up by a white spotlight. The choir, dressed in deep green robes, led the church in Christmas songs.

Jolene and the eight women from the shelter stood in the back row. They listened to the solemn reading as the woman's voice moved out over the congregation. They let the songs fill them up, and a few of them even remembered the words. For some of them, those choruses came to their memory through the years, each song bringing its own images.

Lizzie sat at the end of the row, but she didn't hear the reading or pay attention to the music. She held her thick, winter coat on her lap, and every so often she felt in its pockets to be sure the Christmas cookies she had taken from the kitchen were still there in a small plastic baggie. She rubbed her hand over her jeans pocket, making sure she could still feel the rectangular shape of the two twenty dollar bills folded up, waiting.

Her heart raced as she stood with everyone. When they had entered the church, a kind woman with a crooked smile had handed everyone a small white candle, and now they held their candles, and they waited. The stage lights dimmed as a few people walked down the middle of the church with small lighters and lit the candles of those standing along the center aisle. Those people then passed the flame along.

Lizzie watched as the glow grew and the dark auditorium lit up. A woman across the aisle from her walked over and lit her candle, smiling. Lizzie turned to Penny and lit her candle, and the little flame continued on its way.

Lizzie took a deep breath and released it slowly. She stared at the flame as it flickered, dancing as invisible currents of air moved it this way and that. She stared into the flame, much as she had stared out the dark window the night before, looking for answers.

Lizzie blew out her candle and a small stream of smoke twisted up off the wick. The small pool of wax trembled. She turned to Penny who was already looking at her with questions in her eyes. She handed Penny her candle.

"I have to go to the bathroom," she said. "I'll be right back."

Penny nodded, but a sadness drifted into her eyes.

Lizzie turned quickly, holding her coat, and walked along the back of the church, through the double doors and into the foyer. At the last moment she turned and walked into the women's restroom.

Lizzie stopped in front of the mirror and stared at herself. She stood up straight, wondering what Nae would think when he saw her. She thought she looked much better than when she had last seen him. She leaned closer to the mirror and looked into her own eyes, deep pools filled with so many questions!

Then she heard the door swing open and thud shut. Penny's reflection joined hers in the mirror.

"Hey," Lizzie said nervously.

"Hey," Penny said.

They stood there, not saying anything.

"What are you doing?" Penny asked, and Lizzie knew it wasn't a surface-level question. It was big picture question, the kind of 'What are you doing?' that has to do with the meaning and the purpose of life.

Lizzie sighed.

"I don't know," she said, and she was telling the truth. "I don't know."

Penny nodded.

"Well," she said, "you do what you have to do. You gotta do what you do for you."

She turned to Lizzie, grabbed her by the shoulders and made Lizzie face her. Then she jabbed her index finger in Lizzie's sternum.

"For you," she said.

Lizzie nodded.

Penny walked back out and the door swung closed. The bathroom was silent. Lizzie lifted her jacket and put it on, and she felt the money in her pocket, the cookies in her coat. Then she turned and left the restroom, walked quickly through the foyer, and left the church.

Cold air rushed in where she had been minutes before, and she quickly disappeared into the winter night.

Outside, the night couldn't have been any different from the warm, glowing inside of the church. The slush had frozen along the edge of the road, making it difficult to walk. The wind kept picking up, and she lifted the collar of her coat and tucked her head down in as far as she could. It was difficult to see, except when every so often a car drove by, lighting up the shoulder.

Lizzie walked briskly, almost at an awkward jog, to the nearest gas station and went inside. She walked around for a long time, trying to warm up. She bought a cup of coffee before going out and standing on the sidewalk, her breath bursting out in steaming clouds, the coffee smoking. A few people came and went, but it was Christmas Eve, so there weren't many people out and about.

Lizzie edged towards a tall, thin woman getting out of her car.

"Excuse me, ma'am, I'm looking for a ride to the turnpike?"

"Sorry," she said, walking past Lizzie, staring at the ground.

Lizzie nodded and stepped back, leaning against the store windows. Then she went back inside and wandered through the short aisles again, trying to warm up. Her hands and feet felt numb. A man came around the corner carrying a bottle of soda and a bag of potato chips.

"Excuse me," she said quietly. "I'm looking for a ride to the turnpike."

He shook his head and brushed past her.

She walked quietly to the front of the store, then felt a tap on her shoulder.

"You can't be in here," said a firm voice.

She turned around to find what looked like the store manager. His black name tag said Ben in small white letters. His hair was gelled perfectly and his beard was a small, precise line down each side of his face.

Lizzie lifted her coffee cup.

"I bought something."

"Congratulations," he said. "You bought something."

He turned to the rest of the store and said in a loud voice.

"She bought something!" Then he started a long, slow clap. Then he stopped.

"Get out."

She nodded and walked out the front doors, into the cold, into the dark. Then she heard another voice.

"Where you going?"

This time it was a young girl who looked to be close to Lizzie's age. She wasn't much older than Lizzie. Her face was clean and smooth and her hair was up in a ponytail. She wore black earmuffs and a purple scarf.

"Oh, that's okay," Lizzie said, but the girl interrupted her.

"Seriously! It's Christmas Eve. I don't mind giving you a ride. Where are you going?"

Lizzie shrugged.

"Detroit?"

The girl laughed and said, "That's kind of far."

Lizzie smiled.

"I know."

The two girls stared at each other for a moment. Lizzie wondered if she ever could have been that girl, standing there, drawing close to the end of her high school years, her entire future ahead of her.

"How about to the truck stop just off the turnpike?" Lizzie asked.

The girl's face lit up again.

"Sure. I'd love to."

She walked past Lizzie to a beat-up old VW and got in the driver's side, then leaned over and popped open the passenger-side door.

"Let's go," she said.

CHAPTER FOURTEEN

Running away became a bigger part of Elizabeth's young life. Six years had passed since the police car had rolled up in front of her trailer, six years since the night her mother had never come home. For the most part those six years had been filled with insecurity and uncertainty. Mark Blair had taken any amount of self-worth she had and shredded it. She never felt like she belonged anywhere in this world, so her life became a series of short, difficult journeys without a destination.

Then Roger's nephew Steve came along. His family only came over for birthdays and holidays, but the way he looked at Elizabeth, the inappropriate ways that he allowed his hands to brush against her or the way he always sat so close on the sofa, those things all reminded her over and over again of Mark. She came to despise their visits. She would go for long walks or hide out in her room until her parents came up and retrieved her.

"You can't hide from everyone," Beverly always said,

shaking her head and wondering why this girl had never quite turned out as she had hoped. So Elizabeth would go back downstairs and Steve would stare at her as if he could see inside.

The December before Elizabeth turned 10, Roger and Beverly had decorated the house for Christmas. It was December 23rd. White lights stretched across the roof line and up the peaks. Electric candles shone in every window like so many faraway stars. Even the small maple tree in the front yard had been draped in a cloak of light.

Inside, garlands and wreaths and lights graced every surface. Red bows hung on every door. And the tree, the centerpiece of their Christmas tradition, stretched up to the ceiling in their living room. White lights and red tinsel and all sorts of other decorations wrapped around the tree. As Beverly bought more and more gifts for Roger and Elizabeth and the two boys, she wrapped them and placed them under the tree.

Elizabeth came in from school with nothing but the long Christmas holiday stretching out in front of her. The presents would be nice. She could survive the extra time with her brothers. But Steve: just the thought of him coming to the house filled her with a sense of dread and disgust.

She walked up the stairs and down the hallway. She thought she heard Beverly and Roger talking in their bedroom, and something rose up in her, something she had never experienced before: courage. Perhaps the promise of being ten years old made her feel confident; maybe she had simply reached her breaking point. But she was tired of her life as it was. She was tired of other people crossing boundary lines she tried to redraw again and again.

She knocked on the door.

"Beverly?" she asked quietly.

The door swung open. Beverly looked confused. Elizabeth

had never knocked on her door before, had never even approached without first being approached. In fact, Elizabeth had never been in their bedroom. She felt like she had gone backstage in a play about her life and was meeting the real people and not just the actors.

"Elizabeth?" she asked. "What's wrong?" Roger came over to the door and looked over Beverly's shoulder, questions lining his face.

In that instance, Elizabeth felt something she had never felt before: she felt that someone else was genuinely concerned about her. The look on each of their faces disarmed her, and before she knew it she was weeping.

"Oh my word!" Beverly exclaimed. "Oh, my! Come over here, Elizabeth. Come sit."

She held Elizabeth by the elbow and guided her gently to the bedside. Even before she had sat down, Elizabeth erupted. Words came from her mouth so fast and uncontrolled that at first she didn't even realize that she was the one speaking. But even once she understood what was happening, she released control and let the stories flow.

Before she knew it, she was telling them about Mark Blair and everything that he had done to her. She told them about the first time in the janitor's closet and the many times after that, spaced out over three long years. She was weeping and she covered her face with her hands. She made it through, and she paused, taking deep breaths and sobbing.

"Is there anything else?" Beverly asked in a quiet voice, and if Elizabeth had looked up, she would have seen something in Beverly's face, something that would have discouraged her from continuing. She would have seen confusion and disbelief. But because she didn't look up, because she kept her face in her hands, she started up again, this time telling stories about Roger's nephew Steve, going through the many ways that he made her uncomfortable.

When she finished, she leaned all the way forward and put her elbows on her knees. She didn't want to look up. She couldn't believe she had said all of those things - for so many years they had been stuck inside her, like poison, and speaking had in some ways brought a small sense of healing.

When she finally looked up, it was Roger's face she sought out first, although she wasn't sure why. Perhaps she still hoped to find the love of a father, the kind of love she had seen at that birthday party when she was a little girl, the kind of love that would scoop her up and hold her and squeeze her tight. The kind of love that wouldn't let anything like that happen again.

What she found was a face contorted in confusion and rage. She wanted to look away immediately, but she couldn't. Curiosity kept her gaze, and she wondered what was happening.

"What are you trying to say," he demanded, "that Steve abused you?"

She didn't know how to respond to that. She didn't know how to classify what had happened to her. She was only nine – she only knew how he made her feel.

"Answer me," he said again. "Are you saying that Steve has sexually assaulted you?"

She stared down at the ground. Her eyes flitted back and forth, from the floor to the door to the clock on the dresser, its numbers made up of small red lines. Then she glanced over at Beverly – she was crying, too. But Elizabeth was beginning to think that Beverly wasn't crying for the same reason that she was crying.

"We brought you into this house," Roger said in a controlled voice, "and why? Because we wanted to give you a home."

He stood up and paced back and forth in front of her.

"But you return that with lies? Lies! And when I ask you

questions about these lies, you can't even answer them?"

Elizabeth started to tremble, from her toes all the way up to her shoulders.

"Mark is a good young man – why would you want to ruin his life like this? And Steve? He has it tough, he's never been popular. Why would you tell these stories?"

Then he stopped pacing and he looked at her, waiting for an answer.

Why would you tell these stories?

His question echoed in her mind. She felt just as violated as the first time in the janitor's closet – no, she felt worse, because when that had happened she thought she was alone, but there had always been hope. Now, with Roger and Beverly not believing her, there was no more hope. She had reached the end of the line.

Her tears stopped. The realization that she was alone somehow hardened her. She stood up, as if she remembered there was something she needed to do.

"I hope you don't plan on spreading this any further," Roger said, but she walked away, through the door, back into a life she never could have imagined, back into a life she would do anything to escape from.

Beverly seemed shocked the next day when Elizabeth agreed to go to the mall with her. It was Christmas Eve, and she had a few more items to pick up.

"Sure," Elizabeth said. "Let me get my things."

Beverly stood there staring. When Roger walked through the room, she whispered to him.

"Maybe we've turned the corner with that one," she said. "Maybe she just needed to get all of that stuff out." She said the word "stuff" the same way she would have said a swear word. But Beverly never used words like that.

The drive to the mall was silent. Elizabeth thought back on the scene she had left at the house. The boys had stayed home, complaining about wrapping the gifts they had bought for the rest of the family. Roger had sat quietly at the table, reading a paper, not even looking up when Beverly and Elizabeth passed through the kitchen and into the garage.

That's the last time I ever have to see them, she thought, and it brought both comfort and fear.

Beverly drove the car into the busy parking lot, weaving in and out of other cars that were coming and going.

"Why does everyone wait until the last minute?" she asked under her breath. She was so upset by the traffic that she didn't even notice the small backpack Elizabeth carried with her when they got out and started walking towards the mall.

The day was unseasonably warm for Christmas Eve. With temperatures in the 50s it almost felt like spring, and the ground was wet from recent rains. Tiny rivers ran along the sidewalks and plummeted in miniature waterfalls down into the gutter. Everything seemed to be moving.

Inside, the mall was busy, heaving with people and oversized shopping bags and loud Christmas music. Babies cried and children begged their parents for one more gift and people walked quickly, intent on making that last purchase so they could go home for the holidays. The lines in the food court were long. The line to sit on Santa Claus's lap was even longer.

"Do you want to sit on Santa's lap?" Beverly asked, as she did every year.

"No thank you," Elizabeth replied, as she had every year.

Beverly's eyes became intent as she searched for a particular shop. She was so lost in her shopping that she had started mumbling to herself, her gaze going here and there, back and forth. When Beverly turned and disappeared into a men's clothing store, she never noticed that Elizabeth continued on, straight ahead, never turning this way or that.

She vanished into the crowd.

A few minutes later Elizabeth was outside. A few minutes after that, she was climbing into a strange woman's car, a woman who had believed Elizabeth when she said her parents had never shown up to take her home and could she please give her a ride downtown to Queen Street? And less than ten minutes after that, Elizabeth had purchased a ticket for the bus to Pittsburgh.

She couldn't believe how easy it had been, how quickly it had happened. It was exhilarating, and the whole episode filled her with a sense of excitement and adventure. She had finally left those people! Her only regret was that she had waited so long to run away. If she had known how easy it would be, she would have left years ago.

But she felt a tightness in her chest when she thought about how quickly the money had gone. She had taken $100 from Roger's wallet - in her mind she had "borrowed it" - but after a $59 bus fare and $6 for lunch, she realized she didn't have much margin for error. That money wouldn't last her more than a few days.

She planned on searching for the town where her great-aunt had lived, the one who had taken her to the birthday party years before. She couldn't remember the name of the town, but she thought she'd recognize it if she saw it.

Elizabeth sat silently waiting to board her bus when she first noticed two police officers enter the terminal. Her first thought was to RUN! But if she ran, she would invite their attention. Maybe they weren't looking for her. Maybe they were just there to provide security for travelers. Yes, that's it. They couldn't be looking for her.

One of the officers veered off toward the ticket window to

talk with the lady behind the glass, the lady that had sold Elizabeth her ticket to Pittsburgh. The other officer made a wide circle around the bus terminal and approached the bench where Elizabeth was seated from the rear. Elizabeth avoided eye contact in either direction, but she knew she was being watched. Then the ticket-lady pointed at her while speaking to the first officer!

"Oh no! That woman called the police! She turned me in! I am going to be arrested!" Elizabeth's mind raced.

An inner-voice screamed at her to run but her body did not respond. It was as if she was attached to her seat. She clutched her backpack and hoped that the police officers would just leave, that her bus would soon board and she could escape. But that would not be the case. The policemen moved in from both sides. They stood on either side of her as she sat, looking at her backpack. The older officer finally spoke in a gentle voice, "Elizabeth, you've worried a lot of people today. We need you to come with us. It's time to go home."

Elizabeth stared out the window of the police cruiser as they drove back to her "home." The dark grey winter sky seemed to amplify her sadness. The playgrounds were empty, the trees were leafless, and she felt very alone. Rain started to fall. The drops splattered on the window and streaked toward the rear of the car. She leaned her head against the cold glass. The words of the officer echoed in her mind, "It's time to go home." But Elizabeth had never been "home" at any point in her life.

CHAPTER FIFTEEN

"Thanks," Lizzie said to the girl in the Volkswagon, the girl who had picked her up at the gas station.

"Be safe," the girl said, stopping for a moment and staring at Lizzie, as if she wanted to say something else. Instead, she just gave Lizzie a half-wave and said it again.

"Be safe."

Lizzie nodded, but she knew what she was about to do was about as far from safe as she could get. Not that she hadn't gone around knocking on truck doors before. It was like playing the lottery. She had friends who'd been beaten, raped and left for dead when they went knocking. Then she had friends who found drivers that went out of their way to take them where they were going, even gave them money for food. You just never knew.

The memory of her first time at a truck stop flashed through her mind, how the man she had trusted had taken her there, told her, "I have a friend who can help you get the money you need. He helps girls like you, girls having a hard time."

She shook her head to dissolve the memory in her mind. She didn't need to think about that. She walked around to the back of the truck stop and made her way from cab to cab.

"Not interested," one man said, slamming the door closed.

"Yeah, baby," one man said, his eyes wide, his ball cap barely containing a head of long, greasy hair. She just turned and walked away, and he called after her in a crooning voice.

"Where you going, baby?"

There were those who didn't answer, and those who looked out the window and then went back to sleep. Finally, a man opened his door and looked down to where she stood. He looked like a Grandpa, or a cousin of Santa Claus. He had a round face and a short, trimmed, white beard. His large nose took all the attention from his small gray eyes.

"What do you want?" he asked in a peaceful voice.

"Looking for a ride west," she said hesitantly. Normally nice men like him gave a quick no.

"Where you headed?" he asked again. Nothing moved but his mouth. She kept waiting for his arm to pull the door closed, but he was completely still. She thought she could trust him. He had kind eyes.

"Detroit."

"I'm not going to Detroit," he said, beginning to withdraw.

"Where are you headed, mister?" she asked quickly.

"Wheeling," he said. "Then south."

She thought Wheeling was west.

"Would you take me to Wheeling?" she asked, pulling the bills and change from her pocket, dropping a few coins onto the oily pavement. "I've got, like, thirty dollars."

He took a deep breath and sighed.

"Tell you what," he said. "Come back in an hour. I'm going to get some sleep. Then I'll take you to Wheeling."

She nodded. He closed the door and she got on her hands

119

and knees and searched the cold ground for any coins she might have missed. Then she walked around and leaned against the back of the truck.

She waited.

That's how Lizzie found herself being jolted awake by a large bump in the highway. She wondered how long she had been sleeping and how long they had to Wheeling. The man had refused her money. He hadn't really said much when she climbed in, and as soon as the truck roared to life she had fallen asleep.

She opened her eyes but didn't move. She stared out the window. Heat blasted through the vents, kept her drowsy and comfortable. She wished the drive would never end. She wanted him to just keep driving, keep driving, and then she'd never have to worry about finding another ride to Detroit. She'd never have to worry about what she had left behind or what waited for her in the future. A drive like that would be a never-ending life in the present. No worries. No hope. Nothing.

Then she saw it. She couldn't believe it at first. She closed her eyes imagining that she must still be trapped in a dream. She squinted as if to squeeze the last bit of slumber from her mind. But this was no dream. There in front of her, taped to the dash of this old trucker's semi was a bookmark identical to the one she had received from Miss Jane. As she stared at it, the familiar words seemed to leap from the weathered console.

I am God's child.

I am Christ's friend.

I am free forever from condemnation.

I cannot be separated from the love of God...

One specific statement grabbed her attention. It was almost as if an invisible force had gently, but firmly held her gaze. She couldn't look away. The words almost spoke out loud to her.

I can find grace and mercy in time of need.

"What's in Detroit?" the trucker startled her. His voice was monotone, but there was something comforting in it, as if he knew everything about her but didn't mind.

"A friend," she whispered, her voice barely audible over the rush of the heater.

Lizzie glanced over at the man. He stared ahead at the road, both hands on the wheel. The forward movement of the truck felt irresistible, like some kind of force that couldn't be stopped.

"You ever been there?" she asked.

"Where? Detroit?" he asked, then frowned a disinterested frown and shook his head. "No. Been just about everywhere else, but never Detroit."

The space in between their conversation was filled with the sound of passing cars and the sliding motion of headlights as they moved on down the road.

"You like it there?" he asked.

She thought about that. Did she like it in Detroit? Did she like the dark nights and the mornings so bright she had to sleep with her head under her pillow? Did she like the smells or the sounds of doors opening, cars stopping, people moving?

"It's okay," she said.

He nodded.

"Where are you from?" she asked, trying to be nice to this man who had given her something he didn't have to give.

"Jacksonville, Florida," he said.

"I've never been to Florida," she said.

"Oh, you're not missing much," he said, and then he smiled for the first time. His teeth were straight and narrow and slightly yellow.

"You don't like it there?" she asked.

"It's fine, as far as places go. But I don't much like the beach, and I don't care much for hot weather. I like coming north this time of year. I like the cold."

"I've never really liked the cold," she said.

"It's cold in Detroit, isn't it?"

She nodded.

"Real cold. And windy a lot, too."

"Sounds lovely," he said, smiling again.

"It's okay," she said, shrugging.

After a few more moments of silence he asked her a question she didn't know how to answer.

"So are you running away or running home?"

The question was like a slap in the face. Lizzie stared hard, straight ahead. She thought and thought about how to answer, and she thought so long that the question became irrelevant and soon it evaporated in the moving light and the warm cab.

But the man didn't seem upset by her silence, and he didn't seem to think the question had vanished. He took a deep breath and sighed again. He sighed a lot.

"Usually for me, if I can't answer that question, then I'm running away."

She nodded and the movement of her head came in quick, subtle jerks.

A few miles passed in silence. The green mile markers flashed past them, and in her mind they came too fast, too soon. She willed them to slow down so that she wouldn't have to move forward, so that her life could go on forever on the highway.

Lizzie thought about the girls back at The Hope Center. She wondered what Miss Jolene had done when she realized Lizzie had run off. Had she waited at the church with the van running, the girls stirring in the back seats, or had she seen it coming and driven back without waiting? She wondered if she had called Miss Jane yet and what Miss Jane would think about it, how she would feel about it.

Then she thought about how Penny followed her to the bathroom. Lizzie could almost feel Penny pointing her finger into her chest and the words she had said echoed in her mind.

You gotta do what you do, for you.

The man cleared his throat, then reached down and picked up a cup of coffee that by then must have been cold. He took a long swallow through the hole in the lid, then put the cup down in the holder and cleared his throat again.

"You know why I'm giving you a ride?" he asked.

She froze. That was usually where the proposition came. That was where the talk of "payment" descended. Lizzie shook her head slowly from side to side.

"No, sir," she said.

"I don't give rides to just anyone," he said, pausing, savoring his words. "But with you, I could tell you needed to know there are people in the world who can maybe help you. And I can tell that you need to know there's a God who loves you."

Her eyes teared up and she looked out the passenger side window, coughing in order to clear her throat.

"That's why I'm giving you a ride," he said.

The road fled back beneath the truck, mile after mile, and Lizzie didn't look towards the driver. She wanted to go back to sleep, but she couldn't, so she watched the sideview mirror, hoping for some glimpse of the sunrise.

But they got to Wheeling before the sun came up.

He was the last kind voice she heard on that trip.

It took her two days to make it from Wheeling to Akron. When she couldn't find a ride in Wheeling, she ended up walking about ten miles on the highway and sleeping under an overpass. She smashed herself as far as she could up into the crevice where the road met the cement slabs and she tucked her arms inside her shirt and her coat and she wished the road would crush her. She never even once thought about the fact that Christmas Day had come and gone.

Her sleep came in fits and starts, and every time she woke up she wondered how someone could survive feeling as cold as she felt in that moment. She dreamed of being warm and she dreamed of running, always running, but never fast enough. That was the coldest night of her life, and she almost decided to turn back.

But what do I have to go back to? She wondered to herself. *They wouldn't take me back. Where would I go?*

So she stood up with the sunrise the next morning, shocked she had survived the cold. She stuck out her thumb and found a ride to Akron. Over the next few days she hitched a ride to Cleveland, and from Cleveland she made it to Toledo, and from Toledo she made it to Ann Arbor. Again, she had to walk, and when it started raining a man in a red Chevy pick-up truck gave her a ride to the city limits. He didn't say a word except to ask her where she needed to go.

He pulled off the highway and stopped along a sidewalk. The long street was lined with crumbling buildings and abandoned houses. Lizzie got out of the warm truck and knew she still had a long way to go, but she felt so much closer than she had in Pennsylvania. The rain had stopped but the sky was still gray and everything was covered in a wet sheen. She had spent the forty dollars and her stomach complained - she was so hungry.

Lizzie had lost track of the days and nights in the blur of travel and walking and sleeping and being hungry, but she knew New Year's Eve was only a few days away. She knew she had to find Nae before the end of the year or he'd be gone.

Finally she recognized a few high-rise buildings off in the

distance, and she knew which direction to go. She thought she could be there before nightfall.

A cold rain began to fall again, and she lifted her shoulders, pulled the coat up around her neck. She was almost there.

CHAPTER SIXTEEN

Roger and Beverly gave up on Elizabeth after she ran away that Christmas. By the time she celebrated her tenth birthday, she lived with a different family in a three-bedroom townhouse. The house was wrapped in strong odors: the kitchen smelled of vanilla and the bathroom of bleach. That couple loved her as best they could, in their own way, but they didn't understand that by then Elizabeth had become a runner, an escape artist. She thrived on leaving and on being found.

So after she kept running away, it was with tears and sighs they passed her back. She became a hot potato, tossed around the foster care community, leaving burn marks on the palms of those who caught her, gathering more and more bruises from all the times she was dropped.

By the time she was thirteen, no one knew what to do with her. She came and went as she pleased. No amount of discipline affected her. School was a place she had to endure, and things like grades or detention existed somewhere along the edge of her mind, never acquiring much weight in her decisions. She had the ability to sit quietly and stare into space, visiting some far-off location where no one could find her.

Some days, when she wanted to be alone, she evaded her bus after school and walked three miles to a large, green park. She sat with her back against a massive oak tree and watched the children play and scream while their distracted mothers checked their phones or gabbed to each other. The playground was colorful, especially against the solid backdrop of trees.

In the winter, when the trees were empty, Elizabeth could see down the hill, beyond all the houses, to the highway. She watched the cars and trucks whir past the exit for her town without so much as a sidelong glance, and a desire rose in her to see the rest of the world, to jump into that moving river and let it sweep her away.

The spring after she turned 13 was the first spring she saw the young man jogging through the park. He always stopped for a moment at the water fountain beside the playground and took a long drink, smiled over at the row of reclining mothers, then continued on his jog. He had black hair that was always in place and deep, black eyes.

The only other time she saw him stop, besides at that water fountain, was when he crossed paths with small groups of teenage girls. Then he'd put his hands on his knees, catch his breath and chat with them for a few minutes. He always left them laughing and looking over their shoulders.

But Elizabeth never went to the park with a group. She always went alone.

Spring turned into summer and Elizabeth spent more and more time at the park. Sometimes she took snacks from her foster parents' cupboards and went there for hours at a time, sitting, staring into space, watching the wind move through the leaves.

On a day when the mid-summer heat had emptied the park,

she saw the young man approaching from a long way off. She stood and walked towards the playground, arriving just before he did. She bent over and took a long drink from the fountain. When she looked up, he was standing there.

"Hot, huh?" he asked, going in for a drink.

He was just as handsome as he had been from a distance, but close up there was something off about him, something that filled her with an eerie sense of worry.

For some reason she couldn't speak. She nodded, and off he ran.

After that, she went to the park every day. They started chatting by the fountain. She found out his name was Johnny. He had grown up far away from the small town they lived in now. He worked construction for a small company based in Detroit.

Meanwhile, Elizabeth became more pleasant at home, talking without being coaxed. Her foster parents, enjoying the new Elizabeth, stopped asking her where she went during the day. They assumed, or at least they hoped, that she had found a new friend, that maybe she had turned a corner in her life.

Soon, when the young man saw her sitting under the oak tree, he'd jog over and talk to her for a few minutes. By the end of the summer they spent a good hour talking, almost every day.

"I would do anything not to go back to school," she told him one hot August day while they sat under the oak tree. Johnny's shirt stuck to his body, wet with sweat. He had only just sat down a few moments before, and his breathing was still heavy.

"What's so bad about school?" he asked. She loved how he always asked her questions. No one else ever asked her questions – they just told her what to do.

"What's so bad about school? I don't know anyone," she said. "My teachers hate me. I'm not smart. I don't fit in. It's boring."

She held her open hand up in front of him.

"That's five things," she said. "Should I keep going?"

He laughed and it made her smile. They sat there in silence for a short time. He put his head back against the tree.

"You don't have to go back," he said quietly.

She looked over at him.

"What?"

"You don't have to go back," he said again, this time looking at her.

"Oh, I've tried running away before," she said, her face suddenly sad. "Someone always finds me."

He turned towards her and put his hand down beside hers so that only their fingertips touched. It sent a jolt of something through her, something she had never felt before.

"I could help you run away so that no one would ever find you," he said.

She smiled through her sadness, and she shook her head.

"I'm telling you, it wouldn't work. What would I do about food? A place to stay? I don't have any money. I've thought it all through a hundred times."

She sighed.

"Elizabeth, I'm telling you, I could help you," he said. "I have a friend who can help you get the money you need, find a place to stay. He helps girls like you, girls who need a fresh start."

Something inside Elizabeth came alive at the thought. That's what she needed: help. Just a boost, something to get her started. Then she'd be okay. Once she got out there and started doing her own thing, she'd be fine.

"Would you come with me?" she asked in a shy voice, staring down at the grass growing up between their fingers.

"Of course I will," he said. "Of course."

Silence in the park. The summer sky felt wide open. Anything was possible.

"What do I need to do?" Elizabeth asked.

"Meet me here, tonight. Around 10pm."

"But my parents will still be awake," she said.

"Okay," he said, and by the movement of his eyes she could tell he was thinking, weighing different options. "Make it midnight. Is that late enough?"

She nodded.

"Perfect. I'll see you tonight."

He stood up and stretched his legs. Then he looked at her, smiled, and jogged off into the empty, hot day.

The nighttime darkness was heavy and present, something she could hold in her hands. It mingled with the humidity and the evening heat and was like another layer of clothing that covered up her short shorts and tank top. That darkness comforted her – it felt similar to the darkness inside her, the heaviness that had descended six years before, when she had felt Mark's hands on her shoulders in the unlit janitor's closet.

She carried a small backpack through the night. It didn't have much in it: a few changes of clothing, a small book that had caught her interest, a toothbrush. She had forgotten the toothpaste, realizing it after she had left the house, but she decided not to go back for it. She didn't want to risk waking up her foster parents.

She kept to the shadows and hid behind trees whenever a car's headlights passed by. Once in the park she drifted towards the oak tree. She knew you weren't supposed to be in the park after dark. She wondered if they had some kind of security that made their rounds through the playground and the running paths.

But there was no sign of anyone else. Just the night-time

chirping of insects, and the movement of clouds passing over the moon, the far-off rumble of thunder and the distant roaring of trucks on the freeway.

"Lizzie, over here," a voice said, and she followed it into the shadows.

It was Johnny.

"Hi," she said, suddenly bashful. But he was all business, stern and straightforward.

"I parked two streets over," he said. "Follow me."

He looked different. She had never seen him dressed in anything but his jogging clothes. Now he wore dark jeans and black sneakers, and even though the night was warm he wore a large, bulky sweatshirt with the hood up over his head.

She followed his large stride out of the park and through a dark neighborhood. He opened the passenger door of a small van and she climbed in. He slammed the door closed behind her, and after he climbed into the driver's seat he locked all the doors. The locks made a loud *thunk*.

Johnny pulled the van out into the street and drove slowly past all the dark houses.

"Where are we going?" she asked, but he held up his finger and then answered his cell phone. Light from the small screen lit up his face under his hood, and for a moment she wondered if this was even the same person she had spent so many hours chatting with in the park. He looked much older than she remembered, with dark shadows under his eyes and wrinkles where his mouth closed tight.

"Yeah, she's with me. I'll be right there," he said, and then he hung up without saying good-bye.

"Where are we going?" she asked again.

"A friend of mine is waiting for us."

"Is this the friend you told me about before?" she asked. "The friend who helps girls like me?"

"No," Johnny said, and his words were clipped, and she could tell he didn't want to talk. "This friend will take you to that friend."

"What about you? Aren't you coming, too?"

He stopped the van at an intersection. His headlights lit up the stop sign.

"Listen," he said. "You can get out now or you can trust me. But if you come any further, there's no turning back."

She tried not to cry, but she was scared. She tried to ask another question but her voice caught, and suddenly she didn't feel thirteen anymore. She felt like she was four years old, sitting on the sofa with Mr. Bunny, waiting for her mom to come home.

Johnny sensed her fear.

"Listen," he said quietly, kindness returning to his voice. "There's nothing to worry about. Everything is going to be fine. My friend who we're meeting is a super nice guy. He'll look after you until I can follow you. But if I disappear at the same time as you, how suspicious would that be? I'd have cops from here to Kalamazoo looking for me."

Of course, she thought. *Of course. That makes perfect sense.*

So she nodded and squeezed her backpack tight to her chest.

Everything else happened in a blur. They pulled into the dark corner of a truck stop and Johnny got out and started talking to a trucker through his driver's side window. Then Johnny opened her door and led her to the truck.

"This guy's my friend. He's going to take you where you need to go."

She nodded, suddenly unable to speak. Johnny held her backpack, then helped her up into the truck.

"I'm just going to hang on to this," he said, raising her backpack and smiling. "I'll bring it to you later."

She nodded again, feeling tiny in the massive rig. She wished she had dressed warmer, not because it was cold, but because she wished she had more clothes to hide in. She would have felt more confident if she could have withdrawn into something. Her tank top and shorts left her feeling exposed.

She glanced over at the man in the driver's seat but he didn't even look at her. He wouldn't look at her during the entire twelve-hour drive. Her door slammed and she looked out the window. Johnny jogged the short distance back to his van, scrambled inside, then drove away.

Elizabeth would never see him again. She would never see that backpack again.

The man turned on the truck and it roared to life, loud and intimidating. He eased it slowly out of the parking lot, then on to the highway where it gained momentum. Its acceleration wasn't fast, but it was irresistible.

Elizabeth reached down and held tight to the edge of the seat.

This is how quickly things changed for Elizabeth: one day she was a thirteen-year-old girl eating dinner with her foster parents and worrying about the upcoming school year; the next day she was handcuffed to a bed somewhere in the bowels of Detroit, wondering how life had turned into a living nightmare.

She had met Nae, and he was kind at first. He didn't say much but he knew what to say and how to say it. He had a dark side. He was the one who took her to the room and beat her. He was the one who handcuffed her to the bed. He was the one who gave her the drugs that lit her up bright with wonder and ecstasy and then brought her crashing back to that stinking bed where she was left for a week with hardly any food. One bottle of water per day. A kitchen pot to go to the bathroom in.

She started living for the hits, the highs. She barely experienced her first day on the job, when two of the other girls were responsible for her. She was so high when they took her to the empty apartment complex that it barely registered as man after man came in and out of the room she was in.

Later, completely broken and brainwashed – in other words, when she could be trusted – she'd go to other locations where men would pay for her services and she'd have to do it all without the numbing affect of the drugs. That's when it became too much. That's when she wanted to die.

Days passed, and weeks, and months. In a way that can not be explained, Nae somehow went from being the cruelest person on earth to the one man who truly loved her. He called her Lizzie and brought her gifts. When he gave her a day off, she loved him. She fantasized about running again, but this time with Nae so that she could have him all to herself.

She turned 14 and then 15 and others girls came and went and somehow she wondered if the ones who left were dead but it was a question she never looked straight at. Nae said she was *fine-looking* but she could see her own ribs and her knuckles felt swollen, her skin stretched. Her arms were covered in bruises and she was always sick, always coughing.

Men started complaining about her. She heard them refer to her as "that flea-bag." Sometimes worse. Somehow Nae kept her alive. Somehow Nae kept her going.

"We'll run away soon," Nae said, "Just you and me."

But before that day came, the doors of the house banged open and cops rushed in and girls screamed and shots were fired. Heavy boots thudded through the empty rooms and Lizzie heard the sound of weeping and moaning and cries for help.

Worse than all of those noises, she heard someone shrieking like an animal, some kind of never-ending wail that threatened to shatter glass. Then she realized that the noises came out of her. She was the one making that terrible sound.

And Nae was gone.

One of the cops knelt beside her and put a blanket around her while another walked past. She heard his words echoing towards her through a long tunnel from very far away.

"Hell on earth," he muttered before breaking open a locked closet door and finding another girl inside. "Hell on earth."

CHAPTER SEVENTEEN

But that had been before. Before The Hope Center and Miss Jane and Miss Jolene. Before Penny and decorating for Christmas and that counseling session with the hovering balloon.

That was before, and now Lizzie had found her way back to Detroit. She couldn't quite believe it. She walked the cracked sidewalks in a daze, expecting to wake up, expecting to roll over and discover the smell of bacon frying in The Hope Center. That view of snow drifting down past her window.

When it didn't happen, when the reality of where she was set in, when she walked block after block after block and got closer to downtown, she recognized something in her: disappointment. For the first time since she had fled the church on Christmas Eve, she realized that she wanted to be back at The Hope Center.

But I can't go back now, she thought. *I lost that chance when I walked out the door. Now finding Nae is my only hope.*

The sun had disappeared behind the buildings, and the sky

was losing light fast. Temperatures dropped. A cruel wind yanked at her coat and crept in to bite at her skin wherever it found an opening. She knew she had to find someplace warm to spend the night. Her eyes searched the lengthening shadows.

If only I could find Nae. He'd give me a place to sleep. He'd give me food to eat.

She walked and she walked and soon she entered a more populated part of the city, an area that welcomed the night. Light, drifting out from alleyways, left long slanting lines across streets lined with cars. Brake lights flashed on and off as the traffic stopped and started.

Then, maybe fifty yards up the sidewalk, Lizzie recognized one of Nae's guys. Relief swelled inside her and the night didn't seem so cold. Her pace quickened. Then she noticed the man was arguing with someone, and a small group had already formed on one side, a small audience.

"...come back begging now?" the man shouted. Then he punched the girl standing in front of him. She was a small girl, no more than fifteen or sixteen years old, and she wore a fancy jacket and a short miniskirt that came all the way up around her waist when she hit the ground.

Lizzie stopped in her tracks.

"You can't come crawling back just because you need me, honey!" the man shouted.

"You can't hit me like that!" the girl shouted, and she still had spirit in her voice. She still had some fight left. "I'll tell the cops! I'll tell them about you and all you do."

She spit at him. The man moved like a snake, quick and direct. He slapped her hard then bent down over her, shouting.

"You think they'd believe a 'ho' like you!" he screamed. "Look around! Look around!"

By now an entire crowd had formed, and they joined the

girl in glancing around the street. The streets bustled with pedestrians. People walked by. Some crossed to the other side of the road to avoid the confrontation and the shouting.

"No one cares about you!" the man shouted, suddenly laughing. "You ain't nothin! You can't leave and come back and expect to be treated like a princess."

Lizzie caught her breath and turned slightly to the side so that he wouldn't see her, wouldn't recognize her. She had wanted to ask him about Nae, but now wasn't the time.

"Now get off my street," the man said, turning and walking in Lizzie's direction.

Panic swept through Lizzie like a forest fire. She had to get out of there. She had to find Nae before this man recognized her. He might think she was moving in on his territory with someone else. He might think something worse. Who knows what he'd do. She turned and walked quickly down the street and crossed over to the other side at her first opportunity. Then she stopped.

There, in front of her, leaning against the bright glass of a 24-hour liquor store, was a girl she recognized. Lizzie wandered closer. She couldn't remember the girl's name. Macy? Mandi? Lizzie wondered if she knew where Nae was.

"Hey," Lizzie said, trying to smile, trying to look friendly. "Remember me?"

The girl squinted. There was anger in her eyes, and sadness.

"Should I?" she asked sarcastically.

Lizzie wished she could remember the girls name.

"It's me. Lizzie."

The girl leaned back, glanced away, then looked at her again.

"Lizzie?"

Lizzie nodded.

"Where've you been?" she asked, but she didn't sound very

interested.

"They took me away," Lizzie said, shrugging. "But now I'm back."

"Why'd you come back?" the girl asked, looking around nervously.

"Where's Nae staying these days?" Lizzie asked.

"Nae?" the girl asked. "What do you want with Nae?"

"I'm back," Lizzie said. "I need to find Nae."

"You trying to set me up?" the girl asked, standing up and turning to face Lizzie. "Is that what this is? Cause I'll kill you if you're working for the cops."

"No! Honest. I'm just looking for Nae."

The girl smiled, and it was a crooked line on her face, a leering look.

"Nae," she said, spitting the name out of her mouth.

"What?" Lizzie asked.

"Nae's gone."

"What?"

"Nae's gone," the girl said again, encouraged by the devastation on Lizzie's face.

"What do you mean, gone? Where'd he go?"

The girl shrugged.

"Who knows. Dead? Jail? Hit the road for another city? Who knows."

The girl leaned back against the glass.

"Now get outta here. You're cutting in on my work."

Lizzie nodded and walked past the girl. A strong, icy breeze swept down the street and all Lizzie wanted to do was lie down on the sidewalk and go to sleep, never wake up. Nae was gone. She had nothing. No one. No place to be. No destination.

But somehow she kept moving. Lizzie wandered the streets for hours, past midnight, past the time when all the clubs spilled their customers out into the street, drunk and numb and talking loudly. She leaned against a building and watched the people, so many people, and then, just as quickly as they had appeared, they vanished down the street, and the city grew silent.

She walked and she walked because it was too cold to stop. Her stomach complained and she would have done anything for some food, some water. Even the puddles along the side of the street, dark and wet and nearly frozen, started to look tempting. She heard the loud laughter of rowdy men, a scream and then the skidding sound of feet running on wet pavement.

She ducked back an alleyway and pressed herself against the brick building. Then she slid to a sitting position, hiding in the shadows. The wind had pushed away the clouds, and even through the glow of the city she could see stars in the sky, up beyond the dumpster and the fire escapes.

She thought back through her life, back to the night they took her from her mom. She remembered all the houses she had stayed in, all the couples. She remembered how the man in the park had helped her run away, and she remembered her first stint in the city. Her time with Nae.

That's when she noticed the homeless man sitting on the other side of the alley. She held her breath for a moment. Was he awake? Was he watching her?

"Whatchoo runnin' from?" he asked in a slurred voice.

"Nothing," she said quietly, but he didn't hear her. He thought she was ignoring him.

"I said, whatchoo runnin' from?" he asked again, this time indignant.

"Nothing," she said louder, plunging her hands deeper into her coat pockets.

He just laughed.

"Everybodeez runnin' from sumpin'," he mumbled.

He stood up and walked across the alley, loose in the joints like a scarecrow come alive. His arms swung limp at his side and his knees locked and gave way in random fashion. He sat down beside Lizzie. She still couldn't see his face in the darkness, but she could smell him. He stank of urine and rotten food and sour breath.

"Everybodeez runnin' from sumpin'," he mumbled again, this time louder, and he held up a bottle wrapped in a brown bag, as if to toast her, then took a quick swallow. He sighed with contentment.

"Beautiful. Beautiful," he said in a quiet voice.

"Do you have any food?" she asked, suddenly feeling brave.

He shook his head no, a back and forth movement that eventually turned into a circular motion, as if his head was slowly unscrewing from his shoulders. Instead of saying no, he burped.

"Any water?" she asked. Just saying the word 'water' reminded her how thirsty she was. Her throat ached. Her mouth was dry and her lips, cracked.

"Just this. Better'n water," he said, taking another shot.

"You've got nothing," Lizzie whispered to herself, taking a deep breath and getting ready to leave. The man reached into his pocket and pulled out a five dollar bill. It was torn and stained and barely held together.

"I got nothin'?" he demanded. "I got nothin'? I got this. This ain't nothin'."

Lizzie stared at the bill, twitching and jumping in the cold wind as if it was alive. She could buy a bottle of water and a fair number of snacks with that five dollar bill. She held her hand out, palm up.

"Can I...can I have that?" she asked. She had no idea why she asked. She had never heard of someone like him giving anything to someone like her.

At first he smiled at her hand. Then his smile turned into a quiet chuckle, which turned into a loud laugh, which in the end became a loud, coughing, sensational howl inviting people to look out their windows.

"You're funny," he said, over and over again. "You're funny."

Still, she reached for the bill.

"Please?" she asked.

He snatched it away and stuffed it down into one of his many pockets.

"You gonna do anything for it?"

Immediately she knew what he wanted, and it made her recoil. She felt sick to her stomach just thinking about it. But she also thought about the bottle of water. She'd die soon without water, without food. She had to do it. She shuddered and shoved her hands into her coat pockets. As she did, she felt sharp edge of something familiar poke her right hand.

"Well?" the man asked, impatient.

"Wait," Lizzie said. "Wait."

She reached into the inside pocket of her jacket and there it was: the bookmark Miss Jane had given her. It was folded and bent, but the words were plain to see even in the dimly lit alley.

I am God's child.

I am Christ's friend.

I am free forever from condemnation.

I cannot be separated from the love of God.

And then, further down she found this one again.

I can find grace and mercy in time of need.

How had that gotten in there? She didn't remember taking it out of the small Bible.

What if? She wondered. *What if I go back?*

The idea started small, like a snowflake, but as it churned through her mind it gained traction and began to snowball. Someone had placed the address and phone number for The

Hope Center on a sticker at the bottom of each of those bookmarks, and she stared at it, wondered if she could make it.

"Whatchoo waitin' for?" the man growled beside her.

But her mind was somewhere else. She wondered how long it would take her to walk to the closest truck stop. Should she try to call them first? Would they send someone for her?

Then a burning pain smothered the back of her head. The man had grabbed a fistful of her hair, down at the roots, and he yanked on it so that her face twisted towards the sky. There she saw the stars again. The stars.

"Whatchoo waitin' for?" he demanded again. "I got this five dollar bill here, case you forgot."

"No, I have to go," she began, but he interrupted her.

"You're not goin' no place 'til you give me what you promised," he said, and he squeezed her hair tighter. She cried out.

"No," she said again, squinting her eyes against the pain, "I have to go."

He slammed her head against the brick wall behind them and she almost blacked out. She threw an elbow, her small, bony elbow, and it caught the man in the mouth. He grunted, and for a second he let go of her hair. She jumped to her feet but he grabbed her leg. Her head hurt. A black shadow crept in around the corners of her mind.

He twisted her leg and she fell down. She kicked at him, missed, and hit his bottle. It flew a few feet through the air, out on to the sidewalk, where it shattered.

"That's it," he mumbled, panting with all of the exertion. "Now you done it."

She rolled over and tried to crawl quickly to the street, but he was on top of her now, hitting her, pushing her down, down into the pavement. With each hit she felt her resistance grow weaker. She gathered her strength to fight back once more.

"Scream for help!" she thought, but the drunk's knuckles had stolen her breath.

As she gave in she felt the asphalt absorbing her bruised body. This must be how she would die. Then, from the depths of her soul came a short sentence that spilled out of her mouth in an uncontrollable whisper, "God, please save me."

What happened next was a blur. The man flew off her. There was a loud voice and beam from a searching flashlight. She let out one long sigh, and then she blacked out.

CHAPTER EIGHTEEN

The first thing Elizabeth became aware of was the silence. She didn't open her eyes. She thought she might be dead.

But soon after she noticed the silence, she noticed the pain. There was nothing sharp about it, but it was definitely there, throbbing and solid, out in the edges of her awareness. She sighed, wishing she could expel the pain in that one breath, but it didn't go anywhere. It lingered, and she knew something kept it at bay, something kept that pain from washing over her.

She sighed again and allowed her eyes to open, the smallest crack. She was in a hospital, and that's when she realized the silence was broken by the faraway sound of people walking down a long hallway and carts with smooth-sounding wheels. Hushed voices. A distant beeping.

The door to her room opened and she closed her eyes, not wanting to talk, not wanting to know what had happened. She had brief visions of stars high up above the city lights and a crowd gathered around a girl. She remembered white eyes peering at her across the width of a deserted alley. The bottle made an arc through the air, and she followed its path, its long course through the cold to where it smashed on the sidewalk. She could almost hear the sound of a bottle breaking, the glass shattering on the sidewalk.

Someone made their way around her room. She heard them take something from the foot of her bed, then hang it back on. It made a click as it tapped the metal footboard. She felt the slightest of tugs at her forearm. Cracking her eyes open again, she saw the blurry image of an IV tube where it disappeared into her flesh. She squeezed her eyes shut tight.

The door eased open, the footsteps shuffled lightly out the door, and then the heavy door made a thudding sound, and the latch closed. But by then Elizabeth had already fallen back to sleep, lulled by the quiet and the warm blanket and some inexplicable sense that everything would be okay.

She dreamed of children singing, their voices quiet and friendly.

Happy birthday to you
Happy birthday to you
Happy birthday dear Elizabeth
Happy birthday to you

And she walked into the room but no one was there. Just a piñata hanging from the ceiling, broken open, its contents spilled on the floor. She looked around, and in her dream she knew her father would be there at any moment. Then she realized she wasn't ready to see him – she couldn't figure out exactly why she wasn't ready, but she definitely wasn't ready, so she ran out of the house.

She ran and she ran and she ran.

Then her dream shifted, and she found herself in complete darkness. She knew, without even looking around or being able to see anything, that she was in the janitor's closet at Roger and Beverly's church. Fear overwhelmed her, kept her

146

from being able to talk. She stumbled around the room, looking for the door, looking for the light switch, but in the darkness she couldn't find anything.

She heard the voices again, somewhere there with her in the closet.

Happy birthday to you
Happy birthday to you
Happy birthday dear Elizabeth
Happy birthday to you

She felt a hand on her shoulder, and her heart leaped. She tried to scream, but for some reason, in her dream, she couldn't scream. Air refused to escape from her lungs. Her mouth was stuck, her voice taken. She couldn't move.

Then, in the way dreams can shift and change, she was in the cab with the trucker who had just taken her to Detroit. She looked over at him, and he was kind and he smiled a sad smile at her. He held her hand the way a father does. He didn't say anything for the longest time, but when he spoke, his words came out slow and deep.

"You need to know there's a God who loves you," he said in a calm voice.

She nodded.

Then she was in the alley, fighting the homeless man. He was killing her, slowly killing her, until a bright flash eliminated him and then she knew her father was there with her, her real father. She turned to see him, excitement and relief filling her, and that's when she woke up.

She was so disappointed when she realized it was just a dream. She had so badly wanted to see him. She had so badly wanted to see her father.

The first few days passed in this way. Elizabeth waited, she slept (or pretended to sleep), and she ate and drank when no one was there. The nurses soon discovered that their patient would eat if they left food on the TV tray beside the bed, so that's what they did. Elizabeth was always sound asleep by the time they came back in.

Elizabeth didn't want to talk to anyone. Even though she was feeling better, she was scared. She thought that if she talked to someone, they'd ask her to leave, and where was she going to go? So she avoided talking, even when a counselor came into the room and tried to "wake" her. She simply moaned and refused to open her eyes.

Then one day she heard the door open, and timid-sounding footsteps slid across the room. She heard someone sit down in the chair at the corner of the room, the one the sunlight always shone down on through the oversized windows. The person just sat there. Elizabeth waited. And waited.

I'm sure they'll leave soon, she thought, but minute after minute went by and still she heard the person sitting there, breathing quietly, barely moving. So Elizabeth peeked. Then she squeezed her eyes closed again. She couldn't believe who she had seen.

It was Penny.

Penny from The Hope Center, the same Penny she had always avoided in the hallway, the same Penny who had come to her in the bathroom at the church the night she ran away.

What was Penny doing there? Was she dreaming?

Elizabeth didn't know what to do, so she kept her eyes closed, but she was feeling more and more anxious. Less and less sure of her ability to remain motionless. Just as she was about to open her eyes and say something, she heard Penny stand up and walk to the door. Elizabeth opened her eyes, and she watched Penny leave the room.

But had it really been Penny? Was she absolutely sure?

She looked out the window. She realized she didn't even

know where she was – she had assumed she was still in Detroit somewhere, but seeing Penny made her doubt that. Seeing Penny made her wonder.

The beeping continued. Someone knocked on the door. Elizabeth closed her eyes, and a nurse came in, but this time Elizabeth slept for real, and she slept without dreaming.

Elizabeth came out of that deep sleep so suddenly that she couldn't keep her arms from stretching, her eyes from opening. Who she saw when she opened her eyes surprised her.

A young woman sat in the chair that Penny had sat in. (Had it really been Penny?) Her hands rested on her lap, her head tilted slightly to the side. When Elizabeth made eye contact with her, a huge smile lifted the girl's face, but then, as if trying to cover up her emotion, she toned the smile down a bit.

"Elizabeth?" she asked.

Elizabeth squinted her eyes and tried to remember who this girl was. Her face, she recognized her face, and her voice had a sing-song quality that Elizabeth couldn't place.

"Don't you remember me, Elizabeth?" she asked. "It's me. Dawn. From The Hope Center."

Then Elizabeth remembered. The young intern in the group therapy session. Elizabeth thought back to her words during the session when Elizabeth had scoffed at the idea of God giving good gifts. She felt torn – happy to see a familiar face, yet unsure of what to think about this Dawn girl.

But there was something else, too. Something had changed during her last visit to Detroit, something had softened inside her. She felt open, but to what she still wasn't sure. Friendship with Dawn? A new life? God?

"I remember you," Elizabeth said quietly.

The girl smiled.

"Miss Jolene and Miss Jane sent Penny and me here to see

you. Someone called after you were," her voice paused, then continued, "attacked. They said you were holding this."

Dawn held up the bookmark, and then continued.

"They said you just kept saying 'Hope House' over and over again."

Tears filled Elizabeth's eyes. She didn't remember that but it seemed familiar, as if she had dreamed it.

"So," Dawn continued, "are you okay?"

Elizabeth looked away, not wanting Dawn to see her emotion. But she nodded. Yes, she was okay.

Penny walked into the room.

"Good Lord, girl," Penny exclaimed, walking to Elizabeth's bedside. "You had us worried."

"What are you doing here?" Elizabeth managed to ask Penny. She realized her throat and lips were dry. She wondered if she could have some water.

Without needing to be asked, Penny lifted a glass of water to Elizabeth's lips and let her drink. When Penny spoke, it was in a hushed voice.

"What am I doing here? What am I doing here? Well, I heard you were here, needing someone from The Hope Center. Plus," she added this with a mischievous grin on her face, "I'm all graduated now. Got my own place. Just happened right after Christmas. Woo-wee, you should see it! Got my own bathroom and my own kitchen. I cook something new just about every night I can get new stuff. And I'm going to help out at The Hope Center, at least that's the plan."

Elizabeth stared up at Penny.

"That's wonderful," she said, "but why are you here?"

"What, you don't know yet?"

She looked over at Dawn, who nodded her encouragement.

"Why, we're here to take you back."

Penny looked over at Dawn again, and Dawn looked

carefully at Elizabeth.

"Will you come back with us to The Hope Center?" she asked in a timid voice. "We're willing to give it another try, if you are."

All kinds of warnings shouted in Elizabeth's mind.

You can't trust anyone!

They're just setting you up to hurt you or use you!

They seem nice now but just wait until later – they'll treat you like dirt.

But even with all of those voices screaming in her mind, she stared at Dawn, then at Penny, and she nodded.

"I'd like that," she said.

CHAPTER NINETEEN

Drip. Drip. Drip.

Lizzie opened her eyes and looked around. She was in the same room at The Hope Center, the same room where she had contemplated running away so many times. The same room where she had tucked the money into the window frame.

She felt as though she had traveled through time, or perhaps running away to Detroit had never happened. The hitchhiking, the fight with the homeless man, even the short stint in the hospital: all of it seemed like a dream within a dream. She felt weightless, untethered. For the first time in her entire life, she believed that she could have a fresh start.

Drip. Drip. Drip.

Lizzie looked over at the window, towards the sound of dripping water. The sun glared through the glass. It was a warm day for January, and the snow was melting. The icicles that had formed on the clogged gutters released tiny drops of water that tapped against the siding just outside her room.

She got up out of bed and walked towards the window, stretching her arms and yawning. She had only been back for two days, and this would be her first return to the routine of the house. The part of her that felt weightless, the deepest part of her, found relief in being in the house.

The traffic rushed by on the highway a few hundred yards from the house. All those people, moving. All those stories. It was the first time she could remember staring at a highway and not wishing she was on it, in a car vanishing to somewhere else. Some other place.

She thought back to the dream she had, the dream she kept having. Some of the more sinister elements had faded, but two parts of the dream seemed to happen every night.

There was the part where she was a little girl at an abandoned birthday party. Everyone had already left, and it was just her and a broken piñata. Then came the sound of someone opening the door, and she knew it was her father, her real father, but she realized in that moment she wasn't ready to meet him, so she ran off.

The second part of the dream that she seemed to have every night took place in the alley, the same one she had sat in with the homeless man. Except he wasn't there. She sat with her back against the wall and stared up at the lit windows, and then above them, at the stars. Always in the dream a bright light started coming around the corner, and once again she knew it was her father. This time she was ready, she wanted to meet him, but as the light came around the corner, she woke up.

She didn't want to run from the birthday scene. She didn't want to wake up. She wanted to meet him. She wanted to meet her father. It was perhaps the one clear realization she had, after everything she thought she wanted was proven lacking: she still wanted to meet her father.

She wanted to be loved.

Elizabeth walked over to her dresser and pulled out the small journal Miss Jane had given back to her. She stared at the outside of it, almost frightened to read what she had written before, as if she was eavesdropping on someone else's writing. She opened it slowly and decided not to read back through her old entries. She would simply write starting from that day. Everything that had happened before was gone.

Oh, how she wished that was true.

"Alive" Saturday, 1:15pm

I shouldn't be alive. I should have died in that alley way. I should have died under the abuse of Nae and all those men. I should have died as I continued to run away and live on the streets. I should have died when my mother left. I should have died when my dad abandoned me to my mother's care. All of this time, I have felt so alone. If there was a God, he certainly didn't care enough to notice me. But now, when I think of the danger that has surrounded my life, I am beginning to understand that God was always near. He was always aware. God, I am beginning to realize that you were always there keeping me alive. Even though I couldn't see you in the midst of my pain and loneliness, my eyes are now opened and I am aware you are close. Could it be that there is something good that you have planned for my life? Why else would I still be alive?

Ms. Jane says that now that I have put my faith in Jesus I can expect to hear you and recognize you. But how can I recognize your voice? How can I understand what it is that you want to say to me? This must be how an infant feels when she first awakens to her father's voice. How long will it take before I understand your words? How long before I can talk with you using your words?

Today's verse on my bookmark is from a verse in the Bible in John, Chapter 1: "But to all who did receive him [Jesus], who believed in his name, he gave the right to become children of God" (John 1:12 ESV)

God, I am just learning to believe in you. How can I even begin to think of myself as your child? How can I believe you are my Father? The thought of actually having a dad makes me happy, but are you really a dad? Can I expect you to be excited about me like Justine's dad? Do you want to sweep me off my feet? Do you want to hug and kiss me the way a father does? Can I hug and kiss you? Oh God, if this is possible, then this is what I want. Please be my dad.

As Elizabeth followed the smell of bacon into the kitchen, she also heard something that seemed out of place: the crying of a baby. As soon as she stepped through the doorway she looked around, wondering who was there. Everyone was there, at least all of the girls she remembered from the home, plus Miss Jane and Miss Jolene. Even Dawn was there. Usually breakfast was a simple affair, with only Miss Jolene and the girls. Elizabeth wondered why everyone had shown up.

But she didn't have long to wonder because she soon found the source of the strange sound: a young woman, sat on a chair in the corner of the kitchen, bouncing a baby on her knee. It was obvious this woman was the baby's mother. She had that motherly look about her. She was content to be close to her baby and the baby felt comforted being near *mom*. The baby had glowing red cheeks and round, blue eyes. Elizabeth didn't consider herself a baby person, but there was something about that child that drew her.

"Good morning, Lizzie," Miss Jane said quietly. "Are you hungry?"

"About that," Elizabeth said in a voice just above a mumble. "Could you call me Elizabeth? Please?" The "please" came out as an afterthought, barely audible.

Miss Jane only nodded, smiling a soft smile.

"You've seen our guests?" she asked, gesturing towards the woman and the baby.

Elizabeth nodded.

"This is Carrie. Carrie came into the Hope Center right after we first opened. She loves to stop by and visit when she is in the area and today we get to meet Samantha, her baby girl!"

Elizabeth heard Miss Jane's words, but didn't acknowledge them. She walked straight over to the baby, knelt down in front of her, and stared into her eyes. Something about that baby fascinated her. There was a freshness there, a newness.

"She's so beautiful," Elizabeth whispered, glancing up at Carrie, then quickly back down at the baby. "How old is she?"

"She's a year old, today."

"Today? Well, then. Happy Birthday, beautiful," Elizabeth

said again. She didn't know why she kept whispering. The whole thing felt holy – a new start, a new baby, breakfast back at a place she never thought she'd see again. There was heaviness there, and lightness.

Then the singing started.

Happy birthday to you

Happy birthday to you

Happy birthday, dear Elizabeth and Samantha

(The girls laughed as they tried to include both names, then swept into the last line.)

Happy birthday to you!

Elizabeth paused for a moment. So many memories and emotions flooded over her with that song, with those words. For a second, just a split second, she thought she was dreaming again, or imagining things. But when she turned around and saw Penny standing there, holding a cake, the glow from the candles flashing on her face, she knew it was real.

Today is my birthday? she wondered.

"I completely forgot," Elizabeth said, standing up, a confused look on her face. Everyone laughed nervously, now that she was looking at them, now that she was paying attention. Carrie stood up just behind her and the baby swiped at Elizabeth, grabbing a fistful of hair.

"Ow!" Elizabeth giggled, and everyone laughed again. Now Elizabeth was smiling.

"Hey, you, let go!" Carrie exclaimed.

"So we have the same birthday," Elizabeth said, reaching one hand towards Samantha. The baby responded, grabbed on to her finger and tried to stick it in her mouth. Elizabeth stared at the baby's perfect, tiny fingers. Her thin lips. Her skin was radiant, flawless.

Suddenly Elizabeth felt very aware of her imperfections. Her flaws. Her past. She smiled a sad smile and let go of

Samantha's fingers. Then she moved over towards the cake and took a deep breath, sighing a long sigh.

"I guess you want me to blow them out," she said. All the girls squealed "Yes" and "Of course" and clapped again.

Penny stopped her.

"Wait," Penny said. "Isn't Samantha going to help?"

So Carrie brought the baby over and faced her towards the cake. Elizabeth glanced at her – the candlelight danced in her bright eyes.

"Ready?" she asked the baby, then turned to Penny. "We're ready."

"1...2...3...."

Elizabeth blew the candles out, and everyone cheered so loudly that Samantha started to cry, which resulted in all kinds of attention and fawning and repeated, "It's okay! It's okay!" Penny turned and started cutting the cake. Miss Jane gave Elizabeth a hug.

"Cake for breakfast," Miss Jolene exclaimed. "I never."

The girls laughed and sat down and started eating their cake. But Elizabeth didn't start eating right away. She couldn't take her eyes off of that baby. She couldn't stop wondering what it was that had so captured her imagination.

Then she realized what it was. She saw herself in the baby's beautiful eyes. She saw her new self, reborn. She grieved over the years she had lost, the long spells of loneliness, the terrible abuse she had endured. But she also realized that she had been made new and, like Samantha, could begin again, fresh and lovely. This was a first birthday of sorts for Elizabeth. This was her first birthday as a child of God. She had been reborn and God was drawing her attention to that wonderful reality by sending Samantha and her mom to the party.

She blinked back tears and took a bite of her birthday cake.

Happy Birthday to me, she thought, smiling.

CHAPTER TWENTY

"No More Lies" Monday, 9:45am

I believed so many lies for so long. I thought I was worthless. I thought I was damaged goods. I thought I was simply a bad person God could never love. But perhaps the biggest lie I believed was that God was some kind of distant person who didn't care about me, maybe didn't even know I existed. Kind of like the dad I never met. Then Miss Jane gave me this verse to think about before our next session:

"For I am convinced that neither death, nor life, nor angels, nor rulers, nor things present, nor things to come, nor powers, [39] nor height, nor depth, nor

anything else in all creation, will be able to separate us from the love of God in Christ Jesus our Lord." (Romans 8:38,39)

That's a pretty incredible thing, if you think about it. Nothing, nothing, can separate me from God's love. Which is a little scary because I can't imagine coming face to face with God. My father. I'm going to have to think about that for a little while.

"A Big Day" Thursday, 9:45pm

I am struggling tonight. Tomorrow is the day. Tomorrow I will be taken through The Steps to Freedom in Christ. This will most likely be the longest ongoing session with Ms Jane that I will ever work through.

Ms Jane says The Steps to Freedom in Christ is a tool to help me embrace God's empowering grace in my life and break free from my past, my lingering bad habits. Supposedly, these steps will also help me resist all the negative thoughts that drive a wedge between me and my Father God.

It sounds too good to be true. What if it doesn't work for me? What if going into all the deep places of my wounded heart doesn't bring peace? What if it only increases my sadness?

Father God... you have gotten me this far. Because of the new life I have through Jesus, I can now see that you are with me. You will never let me go. It is still hard for me to trust you at times. Even though I am scared, I want to trust you to bring about my healing. Give me the faith to believe in your plan for freedom.

Lord Jesus, I think of you hanging on the cross. You died for my sin. You took upon yourself the agony of sin, so that through your suffering, a girl like me can be made well. You are no stranger to hurt. If you will be with me, I will follow you to the painful places in my heart so I can be healed, so I might know freedom. Give me strength.

"Something Has Changed" Monday, 9:15am

It's been a week since I've journaled. My freedom appointment with Ms Jane was exhausting. I came away from that experience sort of numb. I wasn't sure what to think. But then something happened. I almost didn't notice the change at first. It was in the group session 4 days ago. Terri spoke without thinking (as usual). She interrupted me while I was sharing. Instead of anger spilling out of me and putting her in her place, I had this unexplainable peace. This gave Ms Jane time to firmly correct Terri in a loving way. Because Ms Jane handled it, Terri admitted her rudeness and apologized to me on the spot! In that moment, I opened my mouth and out came forgiveness. That would have NEVER happened before. Something has changed in me, this time for the good.

I've noticed that the Bible comes alive at times when I read. Sometimes my prayers seem to spring up from my heart and tumble out of my mouth faster than I can think. This is very different. This is very good. I feel alive on the inside. I have peace in my mind. I believe that I am finally free to be the me that God created me to be. Evidently, The Steps to Freedom in Christ helped me finally surrender to God and resist the Devil. My true identity is bound up in Christ and the Devil has run away.

Oh God, my Father, help me to walk in this freedom every day. May I learn to daily surrender to You and to resist the Devil. I invite you to fill me up with your Spirit. I love you. I thank you. I am yours.

"Forgiveness" Sunday, 2:00pm

Forgiveness. Now this is a difficult part of being a Christian. The third step in *The Steps to Freedom in Christ* taught me how to forgive someone in a liberating way. I recall over thirty people on my list that day. One by one, I chose to release them from my bitterness and turn their judgment over to God. In forgiving those people on my list, I recognized that their poor behavior and character was most likely a result of pain they had suffered in life. I even prayed a sincere blessing over people, trusting that God would not excuse any of their sins. God has had mercy on me and I have done some really bad things and hurt many people. Maybe he will choose to do the same for some of them if they surrender to him.

But the memories sometimes return to me. Memories I had forgotten long ago; Things that didn't come up in my freedom appointment. Miss Jane says those memories do not mean that I haven't forgiven. The new memories just reveal that I am growing in my understanding of how the sins of others have negatively impacted my life. When a new memory of hurt surfaces or a familiar memory of pain returns, I have a choice. Through prayer I can talk about the memory with God. I can address the wrong done to me. I can share my feelings openly with God. I can lay the wrongs before God's throne. I am now confident he will deal with those who hurt his children. He might show mercy. He might judge. Either way, I choose to put the matter in his hands and give up thoughts of revenge. I refuse to carry a grudge. This is forgiveness. When I forgive, I am released from the bondage of bitterness and I am free.

Father, thanks for being my great healer and daddy. I suppose if I were to remember all of my pain at once it would crush me. I believe your desire is to mend the deepest parts of my soul. When these memories of pain come, help me not to run away. Give me strength to address my feelings. Help me to talk it out with you. Give me faith to forgive as you forgive.

"Dealing With Flashbacks" Friday, 7:30pm
I have flashbacks of times when I was not using my body in a pure way. I don't think about these

sexual encounters on purpose! But they pop up on the big screen of my mind; my shame plays out in high definition. I'm tempted to feel dirty. I am embarrassed. I wonder what God really thinks of me.

Miss Jane says these flashbacks will come and go and they will lessen over time. That's encouraging, but for now what do I do? Sometimes a very ugly flashback will happen while I am trying to pray or worship or listen to the Word of God being taught.

This is truly a spiritual battle and the enemy of my soul does not fight fair. The battlefield is my mind and with your help Father, I will take every dirty thought captive and let Jesus toss it away. When I am tempted to think that there is something wrong with me, that I am somehow unacceptable or that I am dirty and unclean, I will remind myself... and I will remind the Devil that my Jesus took upon himself all of my sins on the cross, so I can be forgiven and CLEAN!

I am free from my past. Every day is a new opportunity for me to grow in purity. I do this by presenting my body and my mind to God as an expression of love and thankfulness.

I reject the lie that my body is not clean or in any way unacceptable to you, Father. Father God, I thank you that in Christ, I have been made new. I am forgiven and clean. You love me. You love me. What a wonderful thought. I choose to accept myself, and my body, in light of your love. Thank you Father for rescuing me and making me new.

A special verse for me to remember:

Therefore, if anyone is in Christ, they are a new creation.

The old has passed away; behold, the new has come.

(2 Corinthians 5:17)

EPILOGUE

"Yeah, that's true," Elizabeth said, laughing and leaning back in her chair. Miss Jane smiled across the table at her. Outside it was Spring. Spring always returns, even after the harshest winters.

Miss Jane stopped talking and just looked at Elizabeth. Elizabeth could feel her gaze and it was warm and kind and happy for her. They had come a long way in the last months. She felt she still had so far to go.

"Well, Elizabeth, I am so pleased with your progress. How do you feel about things?"

"Good," Elizabeth said. "Actually, I feel blessed. I don't know how I'll ever leave this place, but you've taught me not to look too far ahead, so I'm trying to focus on today."

"Good," Miss Jane said.

She paused and she glanced around the room.

"Elizabeth, do you remember our first meeting?"

Elizabeth nodded, taking a deep breath, letting out a long sigh.

"I do."

"You seemed so scared of life. Of your past. Yourself. You seemed very alone and empty. Today, when I look at you, I don't see a lonely girl. I don't see a scared girl. Do you understand that? Do you see what I see?"

Elizabeth nodded and Miss Jane continued.

"Elizabeth, nothing changed on the outside. You're still at the Hope House. You're still Elizabeth Castle. You're still a girl who lived the life that you lived. What is changing is on the inside."

Elizabeth interrupted.

"You know, I agree with you, Miss Jane. You know I do. But it's not just what happened inside me. It's what happened to all of me."

Miss Jane smiled a surprised smile, enjoying this moment of insight.

"Is that so? Well, what happened to all of you? Did you finally find the Elizabeth you had always been looking for?"

"That's who I thought I was looking for," Elizabeth said. "I thought I needed to get back to who I was before all of this. But recently I realized something."

She paused and looked around the room. Door. Window. Clock.

"I wasn't trying to find Elizabeth. I was trying to find my father."

Both women sat in silence. Elizabeth listened to the rhythmic ticking of the clock, the passing of time, and she smiled.

"And I found him, Miss Jane. I found him because he came looking for me."

"Loving Myself" Tuesday, 2:30pm

Time is passing. Summer is here now. I can smell the flowers in full bloom and the fresh cut grass through the window in my room. I actually love it when my chores include outside work. It feels good to get dirt under my fingernails. It feels good to work hard and to sweat. I love how the air feels clean after a warm rain. I love sitting in the shade of the large trees in the afternoons. It's not like before. I am not alone. God is with me and I have the most wonderful talks with him.

Today Miss Jane told me that God commands me to love myself, not in a way that is filled with pride or "look at me," but in a way that's kind of hard for me to explain. She told me to read 2 Corinthians 6:1 and then go from there.

"As God's co-workers, we urge you not to receive God's grace in vain."

To be honest, I'm not exactly sure what that means. But I think it means that I shouldn't love this new me that God gave me and then that's it. I need to make sure that love that I now have for my new self becomes a love that I feel for others, too.

But that seems like a ways down the road.

Loving myself? That seems like such an incredible thing to do. It makes me nervous to think about myself in such a high manner. But Miss Jane keeps telling me that God loves me, no matter what I did in the past.

Tomorrow we're playing games with the old folks at a local retirement facility. That should be nice.

"I'm a Saint" Tuesday, 9:45pm

The truth blows my mind at times. These identity statements on this old book mark have been so life-giving to me. But there is one statement that is so hard for me to relate to, "I am a saint, a holy one" (Ephesians 1:1). What does it take to even qualify as a saint? Miss Jane says the word "saint" in the Bible actually means "holy one," or a person who has been set apart for a special or holy purpose (Romans 1:7).

I suppose it is an easy mistake to think of a saint as being a perfect person, but that is not true. A saint is a common person who God has made uncommon in identity and mission. Wow! When I trusted in Jesus to be my Savior, something magnificent happened. I was changed. I was given a new nature (2 Corinthians 5:17). I was given eternal life (John 3:16). I received a special purpose to fulfill for God's glory (Ephesians 2:10). Once I was very common, even used up. Then God's grace, through my faith in Jesus, made me holy! Wow... I am a saint! This blows my mind. I can't believe it, but I must. Father God I pray that you help me to believe and understand my true identity. I am a saint! I am a holy one who God has set aside for a special purpose. I want that truth to guide my actions today and every day.

Sometimes I wonder what it would be like to have been born into a normal family. Miss Jane asked me what would have been different? For starters, I doubt that my purity would have been stolen by Mark Blair. I surely wouldn't have given away what was left of my purity by getting mixed up with Nae. Miss Jane recognized the lie in my thinking immediately. She said, "Elizabeth, no one is born pure. You must remember that you were never pure to begin with. Purity is a journey that begins when you trust in Jesus!" That truth changes everything.

With God's help, I can daily commit my body to Him. Nothing in my past can block my journey to purity. In Christ, I'm clean, I know that, and I can move forward.

So I guess I know the truth. I just have to start believing it, and trusting it.

Another day, another important thing learned.

"A Letter To My Father" Sunday, 10:10pm

Dear Dad,

I'm writing you this letter because a good friend of mine, Miss Jane, says it will help me to move on with my life. I'm not so sure, but she has been right before, many times, and I trust her.

Referring to you as "dad" feels strange. I'd prefer to address you as my biological father, since you never really were a dad or a parent. I'll stick with "dad," just because it is easier to write.

Dad, I have to tell you that when I was a little girl I waited for you. Every single day of my life, I waited for you to come to me. Every single time mom took me out, I looked for you. And when you never came home, I started looking for you in my friends' fathers. I started looking for you in the face of every man who ever forced himself on me. I never stopped looking.

It hurt me that you never came back to find me, that you never came back to love me. I thought it

172

meant I was worthless. I thought it meant you didn't love me. I wondered if I was unloveable.

Did you know that boys in my Sunday School abused me? Of course not. You weren't there to protect me. Did you know that day after day I was forced to have sex with men I didn't know, and that I never even saw a penny of the money they paid? Of course not. You never provided for me.

I suppose it is appropriate for me to let you know that I forgive you. You may not even think you need my forgiveness, but forgiveness is as much for me as it is for you. Because God forgives me, I can forgive you, Dad. I've lived long enough to understand that hurt people tend to hurt people. I would guess that you have suffered pain and rejection in your life. Moving on and leaving me behind probably means that you were searching. Maybe you still are. My prayer for you, if you are still alive, is that you realize that the deepest needs of your heart can only be met in Jesus Christ.

Maybe, it all works out for the best. The Bible tells me that all things work for the good for those who love God. I am learning to love God, Dad. I have found him to be everything I hoped you would have been and even more. Knowing God's goodness as my

Heavenly Father makes it possible for me to release you from my bitterness and disappointment.

It's so hard for me to write this letter, Dad, because it means letting go of you. It means saying good-bye, giving up on the thought of your return, giving up on the thought of ever receiving your love. It means cutting ties with the daydreams of what my life could've been like if you were around. But in writing this goodbye letter to you, Dad, I am confessing my hope in God to be my good Daddy and to look after me in all the right ways.

I'm ready to do that. I'm ready to accept that you didn't know how to love me, but that's okay because I have a Daddy in God who does know how to love me. Maybe we'll meet one day in Heaven. I hope that will be the case. I don't imagine I will throw myself at you. I don't imagine I will yell at you in anger. Maybe we'll be able to listen to each other's story and give thanks for God's rescue.

I forgive you, Dad.

I wish you the best.

Good-bye.

Elizabeth

Discussion Questions

The Discussion questions that follow are meant to simply stimulate group discussion or personal reflection. The questions are arranged in a manner that coordinates with chapter sequence and thematic emphasis. Feel free to interject your own questions and observations.

Chapters 1-2

• What is the earliest memory you have of your childhood? How far can you go back?

• Have you ever experienced a fun birthday party? What made it enjoyable for you?

• Elizabeth is a girl with vivid childhood memories. For example, she remembers the details of Justine's birthday party with ease. Why do you think Justine's party made such a lasting impression with Elizabeth?

• Take a minute and think about your most outstanding childhood memories. What emotions are tied to these memories? (For example, as you recall childhood memories, do you have a sense of happiness? Sadness? Fear? Stress? Other?)

• Over time, Elizabeth came to be known as "Lizzie." We pick up on her story as she is undergoing an intake session with Ms. Jane at the Hope Center. Have you ever gone through an intake session? How was it similar to Lizzie's intake session? How was it different?

• What are some emotions you would guess that Lizzie experienced during her first meeting with Ms. Jane?

• Lizzie displays some behavior that gives us an idea of her emotions. For example, she avoids eye contact with Ms. Jane, holds her breath, and squints her eyelids shut. What about you? Have you ever noticed any nervous gestures you have when you are feeling uncertain or nervous? Do you tap your foot? Do you bite your nails? Do you twist your hair? Do you have any behavior in common with Lizzie?

• In your opinion, what is the hardest part about beginning therapy with a new counselor?

Chapters 3-5

• Where did you spend the majority of your childhood?

• Were your mom and dad together during your childhood? If not, who was more present in your life as a child, your mom or your dad?

• Have you ever been in a foster care program? If so, for how long? What was that experience like?

• As a young child, Lizzie spent extended times alone. Her father was not a part of her life and her mother was neglectful. How do you think being alone might impact a young child? Have you ever experienced being alone like Lizzie?

• Some children learn to be brave. Which do you think is more frightening to a child: being left alone by a parent for long periods of time or being removed from your home by strangers in the middle of the night? Explain your answer.

• As we learn more about Lizzie's childhood, it becomes evident that Lizzie has had some very negative experiences with Christianity. How about you? Have you ever been disappointed with Christians or church people? What type of church activities have you participated in? Worship services? Sunday School? Vacation Bible School? Youth group? Other?

• During the follow-up counseling session, Ms. Jane gently asked Lizzie some personal questions about her spiritual beliefs. Specifically, Ms. Jane wanted to know if Lizzie believed in God. She also wanted to understand if Lizzie practiced any sort of religion or spirituality. If Ms. Jane were to ask you the same question about your spiritual beliefs how would you likely answer?

• Hopefully, you too have a copy of the Bible and you've also received the special "Who I am in Christ" bookmark just like Lizzie. Take a minute and look at all the statements that are found on that bookmark. These are a collection of truths that explain the new identity every person can have once they put their trust in Jesus. What one statement stands out most to you? What is it about this statement that draws your attention?

Chapters 6-8

• Try to measure your feelings toward Mr. Sanders. Where does he rank on a scale of 1 (very low/ I don't like him) to 10 (I like him very much). Explain your ranking.

• What about Matthew Blair? Where does Matthew rank on your scale from 1 to 10?

• What might it be like to attend such a strict Sunday School class as a child? Lizzie seems to have been a very adaptable child, but she had great difficulty with Mr. Sanders and her classmates. In your opinion, Why is this the case?

• Why do you think young Lizzie/Elizabeth chooses the closet for her escape? Why not run outside? Why not run to Roger or Elizabeth?

• Has any older person ever startled you like Mark Blair startled Elizabeth? Describe what Elizabeth might have experienced the moment she realized that she was not alone.

• Under Mr. Sanders' teaching, Elizabeth received the following messages about God:
  ○ *God doesn't care about everyone the same.*
  ○ *You can't be good enough for God; not ever.*
  ○ *If you don't do what God tells you to do, He'll strike you dead.*

Have you ever heard these things about God? If so, who told them to you?

• How might Mr. Sanders' teaching have impacted a child like Elizabeth? Can you find any good news or comfort in this type of teaching about God?

• Elizabeth told Roger and Beverly about her understanding of God on the car ride home from church.

Instead of silence, what might have been a better way for Roger or Beverly to respond to Elizabeth's statements?

Chapter 9

• What was the nicest Christmas present you can remember receiving as a child? What made that present so special to you?

• Parents can behave badly at times. Abigail's memory of her favorite Christmas present was stained by her mother's bad behavior, yet during the group session, Abigail relates her Christmas memory to a very special gift she chose to receive in church the previous Sunday: the gift of Jesus. Why do you think some people are able to look back on painful experiences and use them to understand new experiences in a positive way?

• Take a minute and think about Dawn's comments to the group about sin and God's plan for removing sin from our lives. (Feel free to review her remarks in this chapter.) What Dawn is explaining to the group is God's plan of *salvation* or rescue. Have you ever heard the plan of *salvation* explained this way? If not, what stands out most to you about Dawn's explanation?

• How do you think Dawn's explanation of God and *salvation* compares to Mr. Sanders? Which explanation seems more accurate to you? Why?

• When it comes to *salvation* or rescue, where do you currently see yourself? Are you slow to trust in God's plan of salvation? Are you ready to trust in God's salvation for the first time? Have you already received God's special gift of salvation like Abigail described? Where do you currently consider yourself to be with regard to trusting in God for rescue?

Chapter 10

• Unfortunately, the tragic scene that plays out in chapter 10 happens every day. Maybe not in a church closet, but every day girls and even boys are touched and violated in damaging ways.

• After reviewing this chapter, take a minute to recognize your own emotions. What feeling are you most aware of when you think of Mark Blair's evil toward Elizabeth. Anger? Fear? Shame? Stress? Other?

• This is a personal question, but I want you to consider responding: have you ever undergone a similar experience where someone touched you inappropriately and violated your trust? Without going into details, share what that experience was like for you. Specifically, how did you feel after the first time you were mistreated in this manner? Confused? Angry? Sad? Ashamed? Other?

• If you could put your arm around Elizabeth after her abuse at the hands of Mark Blair, what would you tell her?

Chapters 11-13

For many, the pull to go back into abusive situations and oppression is very strong. Even though the Hope Center offers young women a chance for a new beginning with positive outcomes, Lizzie still desires to run away and reunite with Nae (her pimp).

• During the tree decorating, Lizzie develops a fondness for a snow globe. What do you imagine the interior scenery of a busy city represents to Lizzie? What about that snow globe is so appealing to Lizzie?

• In your opinion, why does the idea of change present such a difficulty for someone like Lizzie?

• Lizzie is slow to trust, and for good reason. She had a lifetime full of disappointment. Many people in her life have proven they are not trustworthy. What more do you think, if anything, the girls and leaders of the Hope Center could do to put Lizzie at ease and help her to open up?

The abuse at the hands of Mark continued for some time and Elizabeth found herself isolated, alone and at the mercy of a situation that seemed to be beyond her control or understanding.

• In your opinion, why do you think Elizabeth found it so hard to tell someone about her abuser?

• Chapter 12 describes a birthday party that is very different than the one Elizabeth attended at the beginning of this story. Think a minute about Phil's hurtful remarks.

• In your own words, describe how Elizabeth must have felt when she learned that other kids knew her secret, but wrongly thought she was willingly meeting up with Mark.

• In Chapter 13, a brief but personal conversation takes place between Lizzie and Penny. Lizzie appears to be struggling with her decision to run away from the

Hope Center. Penny says she has found *hope* in Jesus; and more than that, the promise of *freedom*.

• In your mind, what does a free person look like?
• Do you think a person who has been in bondage can easily understand the concept of freedom? Why or why not?
• Penny seems to imply that just because a person has been set free from bondage doesn't mean they will know how to live as a free person. In your opinion, what are the biggest hurdles Lizzie faces when it comes to living in freedom?

Penny later confronts Lizzie in the bathroom of the church as Lizzie is preparing to run. Penny tells Lizzie, *"...you do what you have to do. You gotta do what you do for you... For you,"* she said.

• What do you think Penny means when she gives Lizzie this advice?
• Can you describe a time in your life when you realized that you had been making decisions based on your desire to please others rather than making good choices for yourself?

Chapters 14-15

• Think about Elizabeth's confession to Roger and Beverly. Why do you think Roger and Beverly refused to believe Elizabeth?
• If you could have been in that bedroom, what would you have said to Elizabeth after such an emotional plea for understanding?

- Do you blame Elizabeth for running away? Why or why not?
- In your opinion, is there anywhere an abused child can run to for safety and health? If so, where?
- The encounter with the truck driver is almost too incredible to believe. Yet, those types of Divine appointments happen all the time. If you were Elizabeth, and you awakened in the cab of that truck to find that on the dash in front of you was another "Who I am in Christ" bookmark, what would you think? How would you react?
- Do you think the truck driver should have turned Elizabeth in? Why or why not?
- Is there anything else the truck driver could have done for Elizabeth? If so, what?

Chapter 16

Every day, ruthless people who want to make money at the expense of others prey upon hurting teens. Human traffickers know just how to deceive and trick people like Elizabeth.

- As you read, did you guess what Johnny was really trying to do?
- Who has been the greatest deceiver/liar in your life? Who was your Johnny?
- When people are first trafficked, they are commonly isolated, abused and neglected in order to break their will and brainwash them into obeying their pimp(s).
- Why do you think the initial abuse Elizabeth endured at the hands of Nae was so effective?

• Why do you think trafficked teens like Elizabeth actually begin to develop affection for the person who enslaves them?
• Elizabeth is finally rescued. Do you think she felt like she was rescued? Or do you think she felt like she was being arrested? Explain your answer.
• Are there any similarities between Elizabeth's experience and your experience? If so, what?

Chapters 17-19

Lizzie's determination to return to Nae and the terrible conditions of her captivity might seem bizarre to many, but for those who have been enslaved and abused it is not so strange. "*Stockholm Syndrome*" is a psychological disorder where a victim develops sympathy, respect and, in some cases, even affection for their captor and abuser. The trauma of abuse and captivity has a way of breaking down a victim's resistance to where they ultimately give in and give up. This condition can often be detected when the victim begins to mistake the lack of exceptional cruelty from the abuser as being an expression of kindness. In other words, victims suffering from *Stockholm Syndrome* ignore the injustice and inhumanity of their own suffering and convince themselves to wrongly appreciate their abuser, even believing the bond that exists between them and their abuser is a bond of love.

But what does the Bible teach us about love? From the Bible we learn that God is the source of all true love (1

John 4:7-16) and that God is love (1 John 4:8)! Look at how the bible defines love:

Love is patient and kind. Love is not jealous or boastful or proud or rude. It does not demand its own way. It is not irritable, and it keeps no record of being wronged. It does not rejoice about injustice but rejoices whenever the truth wins out. Love never gives up, never loses faith, is always hopeful, and endures through every circumstance. (1 Corinthians 13:4-8 NLT)

- Given what is known about Nae in the story, do any of his actions qualify as love?
- What about Johnny? Do any of his actions appear loving?
- What about the main characters from Elizabeth's childhood? How many instances do we see them showing true love?
- Now, think about the women and girls at the Hope Center? Look again at the Bible's definition of love. Think about Ms. Jane. How many ways does she demonstrate true love? Think about Penny, in what ways is she loving? Can you name some ways that Miss Jolene demonstrates love?

The Bible tells the story of God's love and his faithful pursuit of runaways. Just like Elizabeth, we all want to run from pain. We try to hide, but deep down inside, we are hoping to be found by someone powerful enough to rescue us and compassionate enough to love us. The Bible clearly identifies this strong and loving rescuer as

God (Romans 5:8). Sometimes it can feel like we're all alone and no one cares. We may think that no one is coming for us, but that is simply not true. Jesus came to seek and save the lost (Luke 19:10). Elizabeth learned the truth at the Hope Center. In chapter 19, Elizabeth journals about God's faithfulness: He was always watching her. guarding her life and keeping her alive.

• Think back over your life. Are there times that you would agree with Elizabeth, times when you knew that God must have been near you and watching over you, otherwise you would not have survived? If so, share an example.

Chapter 20, Epilogue and Final Thoughts

The story of Elizabeth is told in this book for two main reasons:

1. Elizabeth's story gives hope! Regardless of your experience, there are probably some things you share in common with Elizabeth. Elizabeth's turnaround came when she began to realize that God loves her and that God rescued her from human trafficking. But more than that, God offered Elizabeth an opportunity to come out from the enslavement of her sin and be *born again*, or have a fresh, clean spiritual restart. God took great care to place Elizabeth under the authority of special people at the Hope Center who could help her heal from her hurt and teach her to walk in freedom. Elizabeth's story is an example of God's love and his pursuit of every single person; especially those who are trying to hide. There is hope!

2.   This book is meant to prepare you (the reader) to experience a very helpful process called "*The Steps to Freedom in Christ.*" The "*Steps*" have been used by countless people worldwide to break free from the chains that bind up their heart in pain and their minds with lies. The "*Steps*" ultimately helped Elizabeth understand her new identity in Christ. The Steps to Freedom in Christ helped Elizabeth move from being a victim to a victorious Christian. You too can experience this victory in Christ by going through the "*Steps*". *The Steps to Freedom in Christ* is an important therapy tool that will help you begin your new journey as a free person with confidence.

After finishing this book, take the time to talk to your facilitator/counselor/group leader/case worker about going through *The Steps to Freedom in Christ*. God desires for you to be free. Freedom allows you to be the you that God created you to be! Make plans today for your *Freedom Appointment* where you will be guided through *The Steps to Freedom in Christ*.

Finally, may the God of the Bible, our Heavenly Father, guide you and bless you in your recovery and healing. May you find strength to keep moving forward. May your setbacks be few and your victories be sure. May you daily be reminded of God's great love for you. May you grow to learn that you are not defined by your mistakes or the hardships you have suffered but by your Creator God who has made a way for you to have new life through Jesus Christ.

If you are reading this book on your own (not as a part of any treatment plan) and you would like more information on how to be free in Christ, please check out the Freedom in Christ Ministries website: *www.ficm.org*. There you will find resources and contact information for people who can help.

Grace and peace to you.

Who I am in Christ

I am accepted.

I am a child of God. (John 1:12)
I am Jesus' chosen friend. (John 15:15)
I am holy and acceptable to God. (Rom. 5:1)
I am united to the Lord and am one spirit with Him. (1 Cor. 3:16)
I have been purchased with a price. I now belong to God. (1 Cor. 6:19, 20)
I am a part of Christ's body, part of His family. (1 Cor. 12:27)
I am a saint, a holy one. (Eph. 1:1)
I have been adopted as God's child. (Eph. 1:5)I have been bought back (redeemed) and forgiven of all my sins. (Col. 1:14)
I am complete in Christ. (Col. 2:10)

I am secure.

I am free forever from punishment. (Rom. 8:1-2)
I am sure all things work together for good. (Rom. 8:28)
I am free from any condemning charges against me. (Rom. 8:31f)
I cannot be separated from the love of God. (Rom. 8:35)
I am hidden with Christ in God. (Col. 3:3)
I am sure that the good work that God has started in me will be finished. (Phil 1:6)
I am a citizen of heaven with the rest of God's family. (Eph. 2:19)
I can find grace and mercy in times of need. (Heb. 4:16)
I am born of God and the evil one cannot touch me. (1 John 5:18)

I am significant.

I am salt and light for everyone around me. (Matt. 5:13,14)
I am part of the true vine, joined to Christ and able to produce lots of fruit. (John 15:1, 5)
I am hand-picked by Jesus to bear fruit. (John 15:16)
I am a Spirit-empowered witness of Jesus Christ. (Acts 1:8)
I am a temple where the Holy Spirit lives. (1 Cor. 3:16; 6:19)
I am at peace with God and He has given me the work of making peace between Himself and other people. (2 Cor. 5:17f.)
I am God's co-worker. (2 Cor. 6:1)
Even though I live on earth, I am actually one with Christ in heaven. (Eph. 2:6)
I am God's special project, His handiwork, created to do His work. (Eph. 2:10)
I am able to do all things through Christ who gives me strength! (Phil. 4:13)

Kalleah M

Kalilah N

Kalil -(Ka-lil)